PALO DURO

-A THRILLER-

ANDREW J BRANDT

BLUE HANDLE PUBLISHING
AMARILLO

ALSO BY ANDREW J BRANDT:

THE TREEHOUSE

THE ABDUCTION OF SARAH PHILLIPS

IN THE FOG

AMERICAN ATONEMENT (NOV 2020)

MIXTAPE FOR THE END OF THE WORLD (MAY 2021)

ANDREW J BRANDT

PALO DURO

-A THRILLER-

Blue Handle Publishing
Amarillo, TX

Copyright © 2020 Andrew J Brandt

All rights reserved, including the right to reproduce this book or any portions thereof in any form whatsoever. For information, address:
Blue Handle Publishing 2608 Wolflin #963 Amarillo, TX 79109

Second edition June 2020

For information about bulk, educational and other special discounts, please contact Blue Handle Publishing.

Caprock Publishing Group can bring Andrew J Brandt to your live event. For more information or to book an event, contact Blue Handle Publishing.
www.bluehandlepublishing.com

Cover & Interior Design: Caprock Concepts
Editing: Brandon Biggers

ISBN: 978-1-7352206-1-1

PRAISE FOR
ANDREW J BRANDT

"[*Palo Duro*] makes me want to throw on my hiking shoes & fill up my water for a hike. You'll love the magic of the canyon Andrew J Brandt reveals."

—Niccole Caan, *KVII-TV ABC7 Amarillo*

"[*In the Fog* is] an engrossing supernatural thriller...with a dash of *Lord of the Flies* thrown in for measure."

—PenCraft Award-winning author Rick Treon

"[*The Treehouse*] is the next *Stand By Me!*"

—Dusty Boyd, *CBS Radio*

"The highlight [of *Palo Duro*] was Brandt's use of place—the scenery so evocative. The setting and the way he incorporated it into the story brought to mind the greats like Nevada Barr and Tony Hillerman. I highly recommend it!"

—Danielle Girard, *USA Today* Bestselling author

"[*In The Fog* is] the sort of story that begs to be read with a whiskey and a blanket on cold winter evenings...a welcome addition to the library."

—Derek Porterfield, author of *No-Mod*

"[*The Abduction of Sarah Phillips*] grabbed me by the collar and wouldn't let go…with some of those 'WTF' moments that I live for."

—Nicole Reeves, author of *Crimson Hearts*

"[*Palo Duro*] is a modern-day episode of *The Twilight Zone*. I couldn't put it down!"

—Mark R. Hopkins, author of *Deceit: A Life of Lies*

ANDREW J BRANDT

For Jennifer, who said yes to a lifetime of adventure.

PALO DURO: A THRILLER

If you've purchased any of my books; if you've taken your hard-earned dollars and spent them on an Andrew J Brandt novel and I was able to take that money and pay my electric bill, I am more indebted to you than I could possibly put into words here. To every single one of you—thank you, from the bottom of my heart.

This one is dedicated to you.

PALO DURO: A THRILLER

AUTHOR'S NOTE

Palo Duro Canyon is a real place. I've been there countless times in the last fifteen years that I've lived in the Texas panhandle. The gorgeous views and the way the canyon opens up in the otherwise flat plains of the area is astounding. It also has its dangers. Flash floods rip through the river that runs through the canyon every time there's a storm. There are cacti, rattlesnakes and coyotes. But there is also an immeasurable amount of history there. From the Native Americans to Charles Goodnight and the first ranchers to New Deal-era trails and relics, there's more to the canyon than I could possibly write here. Though this story is a work of fiction, I've tried my best to add flourishes of real life in the pages. Beyond being a thriller —that I hope you enjoy — it's very much a love letter to my adopted home. The city of Canyon is a real place, as is the university there. You'll also find bits of the area that I took some creative license with. But that's a great thing about being a writer. It's not always true, even if you're writing the truth.

-Andrew J. Brandt
1 Feb 2020

PART ONE

PALO DURO: A THRILLER

PROLOGUE

RACHEL HERNANDEZ KNEW she was in trouble. As the sun sank just below the horizon line, the night air cooling to the point that she had to zip up her orange down jacket to keep warm, she needed to head back to her vehicle as soon as possible. The last thing she wanted was to be out here on the trails after it got dark. In fact, if her brother found out she was out here alone—much less alone at this hour—he would tell her how *stupid* she was, probably loud enough for the entire campus to hear.

Rachel and Ricardo (Ricky, he preferred, though their mother always called him by his full name *Ricardo Joseph Hernandez* when he was in trouble) were twins, sophomores at West Texas A&M University, and like a lot of twins, they couldn't be more different from one another. One was pragmatic and calculated, while the other was free-spirited with a head in the clouds and a penchant for imagination and exploration. With one of them alone in the canyon at dusk, searching for Native American artifacts, you can probably guess which was which.

Rachel, an anthropological student at the university, was both fascinated by and curious about the ancient Native American civilizations that once inhabited the valley of Palo Duro Canyon, long before Francisco Coronado and the *conquistadors* traipsed all through the Texas panhandle in the 1500's. In fact, it was her love of all things Native American that drove her to attend West Texas A&M in the first place. With Palo Duro Canyon just twenty miles from the campus, she spent most of her free time down here, usually with her roommate Jordan and a few other students in the anthropology program, searching for signs of ancient encampments and a civilization that was wiped out when the Europeans infiltrated the land.

The canyon carved a hole into the otherwise flat Texas panhandle nearly twenty miles wide at some points and almost a thousand feet deep. The elements had formed, over thousands of years, various formations that struck Rachel in wonder. From the sandstone hoodoos to the sheer cliffs cut by millions of years of weather and change, the whole thing fascinated her. And while she loved to spend time down here in "the Grand Canyon of Texas," her brother spent most of his time in the computer lab.

It never ceased to amaze Rachel—two kids from the same parents, same genes, who couldn't be more identical, were complete opposites. In fact, she had found him in the I.T. lab before she drove to the canyon earlier that morning. He was working on some piece of equipment, some experiment that held his entire attention while she had told him, voice full of wonder and eyes wide with imagination, what she was going to look for.

"Somewhere in the caves there are ancient dwellings," she had said. "From when the Kiowa lived in the canyon, before Coronado arrived. They were driven out by other tribes later, but allegedly, there's still some dwellings where the paintings and carvings haven't been altered. I was down there last week and I found a new entrance to the cave system. I think that's where they are."

Ricky had kind of *hhhhmph*'ed as he soldered together the components of the strange device.

"Are you even listening?" she asked him, perturbed.

"Mmmhmm," he said, preoccupied, his eyes never coming up from the device. Strands of his long hair coming loose from behind his ear fell into his line of sight and he pushed it back. "Cave dwellings."

"Right! Does that not excite you? Can you imagine what kind of history is there, just waiting to be discovered? Dr. Errington said she's been looking for them for twenty years," she said, her voice quickening as she paced the laboratory floor. "And, look," Rachel produced a map, photocopied from a handwritten original that looked like it was several centuries old. "According to this, those caves are close to an ancient landslide, hidden by some boulders. Hard to access, easy to defend from attackers. I overlaid a present-day map over this, and it's on some private land, near the boulder garden trail."

"That's great, but do you know what excites me, Rach?" he said as he clapped his hands together and stood back from his device. "This." He pushed a button on the thing and it hummed to life. Suddenly, the sounds of the band Snow Patrol came from multiple speakers mounted on the workbench in the room.

"Music?" she asked, confused.

"Not just music, Rach. Check it out. This Linux server can stream the same source to multiple speakers. Whole-dorm audio," Ricky said. On a control panel on the front of the computer's casing, he flipped a dial and the song changed to another.

"You already have Bluetooth speakers," Rachel

said, rolling her eyes. This electronic tinkering, spending countless hours surrounded by countless pieces of technology, was not anything new. Rachel would go absolutely stir-crazy being indoors as much as Ricky was as he worked on these various projects. There was too much beauty and wonder and majesty outside for her to be cooped up all day in some electronic laboratory.

"This isn't just regular Bluetooth. Pull out your phone," Ricky said, and she obliged. "Now, open up your music. You should see an icon at the bottom of the screen for Bluetooth play. Click it."

Rachel selected a song and then selected this new icon at the bottom of her screen. "It's not doing anything," she said. "Your machine doesn't work." The last two words were succinct and almost sarcastic.

"That's what you don't get," Ricky said. "It's a multi-device jukebox. We can put this in the dorm and anyone can attach their own speakers to the network and then play whatever they want, and it all goes into a queue. It's open-source radio! Everyone gets to create a never-ending playlist and you can attach your phone and your own speaker to the mesh."

"Oh wow," Rachel said. "That is kind of...cool."

"See? I can be cool sometimes," he said with a smile.

Rachel laughed. "No, I said *this*," she pointed at the

device, "is cool. *You* still have a long way to go."

"So is your roommate—what's her name?"

"*Jordan,*" Rachel cut him off. He didn't have to pretend to be ignorant; he knew exactly what her name was. Rachel had caught her brother staring at her roommate more than once, his eyes glassed over with the look of dreamy infatuation.

"Right. Jordan. Is she going with you?" On the workbench, Ricky pulled a monitor that hung on a wall-mounted arm in front of him and started typing. Lines of code, none of it intelligible to Rachel, blurred on the screen.

"Um, yeah," she lied.

"Good. You know mom doesn't like it when you go down there by yourself," Ricky said.

"Well, I'm not. And even if I was, Mom doesn't have to know. Besides, I won't be gone long." She looked at her wristwatch, a Timex Expedition she'd received as a birthday gift from their mother a few years ago. The back had an inscription, etched into the stainless steel. *Not all who wander are lost*, it read. The luminescent hands on the dial, glowing in the low light of the tech lab, read a quarter past three. "I'm going to take a few pictures once I get to the caves and come right back."

"Alright," he said warily. "Be careful. There's Sasquatches down there."

"Oh my god, Ricky," she said. "There's no such thing as a damn Sasquatch."

And with that she had left the lab, went to her car, and drove down to the canyon. Now, nearly five hours later, she found herself off the main trails, the sun quickly going down. She knew Ricky would throw a fit. He'd probably even tell their mother that she was down there well past sunset, if he hadn't already. Despite being nineteen years old, she still felt like a little girl in her mother's eyes.

Now she whacked her way through the brush, trying to find the trail that would take her back to the trailhead parking lot. She had just been on it, the little dirt path that cut through the mesquite brush. How had she wandered off of it? Despite her hurry, she felt an immense satisfaction with the day trip. She'd found the caves. Hundreds of paintings, depictions of ancient Native life, adorned the walls. She thought they'd be worn over time, of course, but, no. They were still there in all their black and gold glory and as if they'd been etched that very day. She had taken several pictures and written down the coordinates of the cave in her black Moleskine notebook. Doctor Errington, the head of the anthropology department, would be so excited when she'd shown her what she'd found. Who even knew when the last time it was that a human actually laid eyes on these cave paintings?

Turning around a large bush, something caught her attention. As the bushes rustled ahead of her, she turned on her light and saw the hulking figure in the brush. It was a bison, no more than forty yards ahead of her. She couldn't believe it. Taking out her phone, she snapped a couple of pictures of the creature as it grazed on some grass, seemingly paying the girl no mind. Rachel couldn't wait to show Dr. Errington and Jordan all the pictures from this day trip.

Off in the distance, past the grazing bison, smoke softly billowed above the mesquite brush from an encampment a few hundred yards ahead of her. She realized that it was now almost completely dark. The sun had set faster than she'd anticipated and the group of tents was lit by fires, a soft orange glow casting silhouettes in the dark. From here, she could make out four tents poking above the canyon floor, cutting into the quickly-darkening sky.

Rachel knew there were backpacking and primitive campsites in the canyon, but they were generally further down the river that ran through the canyon, on the south side of the state park. This didn't look like a primitive campsite, however. In fact, as she observed the encampment through the brush, she saw several more tents a little further back, their tops peeking through in the distance.

She took out her phone and began taking photographs, zooming in on the encampment. It was unlike anything she'd ever seen, but also so familiar. Rachel realized what she was seeing—they weren't tents, but *teepees*. She'd never seen historically-authentic teepees in person before out in the wilderness. She wondered if there was a historical reenactment event going on.

Before she had time to react, a sound, the crunching of branches on dirt, from behind startled her. In her fascination, Rachel never saw the person come up behind her. She felt a pair of strong hands wrap around her mouth and she tried to scream, tried to kick, but multiple arms were around her now as she was dragged off the trail and into the night.

CHAPTER ONE

"I DON'T KNOW. I think around three, maybe four o'clock. No, definitely not four because I left the lab before then. Yeah, probably closer to three." Ricky explained to Jordan. "But you're saying you didn't go with her?"

"No, she told me she was going, but I had a lot of studying to do so I stayed here," Rachel's roommate said. Jordan Harris was tall and lanky with a fluidity in her movements that captivated Ricky and skin that glowed with a caramel richness. Her hair, curly black tresses, fell in every direction around her face, framing her strong jaw. Ricky could barely hide his infatuation with her, though he doubted she'd even notice.

"She lied to me, then," Ricky said.

He'd gone to their dorm when he didn't hear back from her that evening. It was completely dark now, the stars glowing like holes in a canopy above the campus as he walked to the wing of the building where his sister lived with Jordan.

Ricky continued, "She'd told me you were going with her." He was incensed.

"Well, have you tried calling her?" Jordan asked, pulling her phone from the waistband of her black skin tight lululemon pants and thumbing at the device.

"Of course I did," Ricky said. "But apparently there's no cell service once you're down in the canyon."

"Oh, yes. You're right. There aren't any towers down there. You have to go back to the entrance to get cell signal. Do you want to drive out there, see if we can find her?" the girl asked.

Ricky thought about it for a moment and then nodded. "Yes I do, actually."

He couldn't believe how irresponsible Rachel had been, going down to the canyon alone, especially this late in the afternoon. He was a natural worrier, full of tension and anxiety, and his sister's free-spiritedness made his heart and head hurt. Even now, he could feel his pulse rising, the blood pumping through his body at a quicker rate every minute.

They had always been this way, from the time they

were little. She would pester him to jump off the top of the slide on the playground across the street from their house, to catch bugs and lizards in the dirt. When they were teenagers, it was Rachel who wrecked their shared vehicle. He was too scared to even drive on the highway.

Instead, Ricky Hernandez found himself fascinated with technology, learning how to code and build computers. He'd built his first computer, a flat black desktop tower that ran Windows 7, with his father's help— a year before the man died from a sudden heart attack at the youthful age of forty-eight—when he was just fourteen years old. He'd joined the robotics club at their high school where he won a national scholarship for the automation software that they'd compiled for the GPS-navigation drone they'd built.

For college, he wanted to go to Cal Tech, or Arizona State, somewhere far away from the monotony and small-mindedness of small-town Texas. Instead, he'd accepted the scholarships to West Texas A&M. In the end, he realized that he couldn't be far from home.

He wanted it, though. There was a part of Ricky that despised the anxiety, the lack of confidence. And deep down, if he had to be honest, he was jealous of Rachel, that she was so unbound and free. He'd give almost anything to be more like her sometimes.

In this moment, however, that jealousy was far from

his mind, replaced only with anxiety and fear.

And indignation.

Righteous indignation, brought on by Rachel's seeming inability to take others into consideration when she just went off into the canyon by herself.

Pulling out his own iPhone, he tried to track Rachel's location once again, showing only her last known location at the entrance to the canyon before she lost cell service.

"You'll go with me?" he asked Jordan, though she was already pulling on a pair of tennis shoes and a maroon hoodie.

"Of course I will. Who knows, maybe she got a flat tire or something." Looking up, she noticed the unsettled look on Ricky's face. "It's going to be okay, Ricky. She's a big girl, you know." She grabbed her car keys off the desk next to her bed.

"I'm just worried because she went down there by herself. I don't know why she'd do that," Ricky said.

"Well, she did ask me to go," Jordan said. "But like I said, I had a lot of studying to do before midterms, and I still have to write a paper for Doctor Errington."

He looked at his watch. It was now nearly eight thirty, which meant it would be close to nine o'clock before they would get to the canyon entrance. "Thanks for coming with me," he said as they left the dorm and walked the hallway to the parking lot.

"Of course," she said. "Besides, I'm sure I know the trails and where she'd go much better than you."

Ricky's ears burned red with embarrassment. He'd only gone down there once, when their mother had driven them up to the school for a tour. They'd spent half a day hiking some popular trail. That had been over three years ago, however.

"No offense," she said.

"No, I get it," Ricky said curtly.

They reached Jordan's car, a sleek and new Toyota Rav4, and Ricky got in the passenger's seat.

When Rachel and Jordan met just before their collective freshman year at the university, they were immediate best friends. Ricky wished he'd had that kind of connection with someone else, a friend that he could spend time with, who could understand him. The technology department, however, was inherently an antisocial one.

You don't need friends to type code or build a dorm-wide Bluetooth jukebox.

The drive took about twenty minutes and they pulled up to the gate entrance to the state park. A park ranger, who looked young enough that he could have passed for a student at the university himself, propped open the sliding window in the shack attached to the gate.

"Y'all are probably the last ones in for the night,"

he said.

"We're not staying," Jordan said through her rolled-down window. "Our friend—well, *his* sister, my friend—came down earlier today and we're coming to get her."

The park ranger furrowed his brow, creating lines in the forehead of his otherwise youthful face. "Everything alright?"

Ricky started, but Jordan put her hand on his leg. That shut him up real quick. "Yes, we're sure she's fine. She probably got her car stuck down there and couldn't call out because of the cellphones."

"Mmmhmm," the ranger mumbled. "Do you know where she went?"

Jordan thought for a moment. "I do, actually. She went looking for some cave dwellings and pictographs that she thought may exist somewhere near the boulder gardens."

"Oh yes, I know what you're talking about," the ranger said. "We get that sometimes, kids looking for some fabled cave." The boulder garden in Palo Duro canyon was the remnant of a prehistoric landslide that left dozens of large, climbable rocks strewn about in an area of the valley. "I'm going to follow you down to the floor, just to make sure everything's alright."

He waved them through and Jordan drove over the hump in the road past the gate. She slowed down for a moment to wait for the park ranger and once she saw his headlights behind them, she started down the winding road that hugged the canyon wall and led down to the bottom. The autumn sunsets in the Texas panhandle would regularly wash the evenings in a beautiful array of pink and golden hues, giving way to dark blue and midnight skies. As Jordan drove her Toyota down to the canyon floor, the only light visible now was from the stars shining above them. As they descended further, the SUV's transmission revving as they weaved the road, fewer and fewer of the stars could be seen, the vast horizon blocked by the thousand-foot walls of the sandstone canyon.

"I don't understand what you girls get out of coming down here," Ricky said. "It's just a bunch of *dirt*."

"Oh, come on," Jordan said. "Maybe if you came out of the tech lab from time to time and got some fresh air, you'd appreciate the beauty of this place. It's not just dirt. It's millions of years of evolution, of geologic changes and human history. Plus, it's just gorgeous. Georgia O'Keeffe used to paint pictures of this place. Sometimes I even find it hard to believe that it exists. The entire panhandle is so flat and then all of a sudden, this gorgeous canyon just opens up before your eyes. I can't even imagine what the Spanish thought when they first saw it."

"Hmm," he said, still unimpressed. "Let's just find

Rachel so we can get back to campus. I don't like that it's so dark out here."

Once they reached the bottom of the canyon, the road widened slightly and they crossed a bridge over the Prairie Dog Town Fork of the Red River, the flowing water that etched the canyon over the course of millions of years. Off in the distance, capitol peak rose like a sandstone dome, illuminated by the unadulterated glow of the night sky.

"The stars out here," Ricky said, looking out the window. "You can see so many of them."

"It's really pretty out here at night," Jordan agreed.

"Where are these—what did you call it? Rock gardens?" Ricky asked.

"The boulder gardens, they're just up ahead, after the next river crossing," she answered. "Most of this is open to the public, part of the state park. But just beyond the boulder garden is the cut-off."

"I can't believe she came out here alone. Look at this," Ricky said. "Anything could go wrong."

Jordan looked at him, trying to ease his concern. "It's okay, I promise. She's fine."

But Ricky didn't feel fine. He felt an unease in the pit of his stomach that he didn't want to acknowledge. Acknowledgement meant acceptance, and he wasn't sure yet that he wanted to accept that this whole thing felt *off* to him, in a way that only made sense in his brain yet couldn't articulate.

When he and Rachel were younger and growing up in Decker, a small town in the Texas hill country, Rachel broke her arm the summer before second grade while climbing a tree and Ricky swore he could feel the pain in his own arm. The girl had a bright pink cast, slowly covered in Sharpie marker from various people signing it all summer, and at night, Ricky would lay in bed and could actually feel his own arm throbbing. Their mother, of course, said it was all in his head, but as they grew up, Ricky always felt this unexplainable connection with Rachel that defied logic and science.

As he sat in the passenger seat of Jordan's Toyota, coming up on the trailhead where the boulder gardens sat in the canyon, he felt that same tingling that he'd felt in his arm as a seven-year-old kid, now at the base of his neck. It sent shivers down his spine, causing him to shift uncomfortably in his seat.

The road curved once more and a dirt parking area opened up to the right of the path, empty except for one vehicle. Ricky knew immediately — he could pick out the blue Subaru from a lineup of a hundred cars, with its 26.2 bumper sticker that she'd slapped on after her first marathon in Dallas and West Texas A&M parking pass stuck to the back window. The vehicle was dark, empty and abandoned.

"That's her car," Jordan said, but he already knew.

Ricky sat in silence, the Toyota coming to a halt behind his sister's vehicle. The tingling remained at the base of his neck, radiating cold shivers down his spine.

"She's still out here somewhere," he said.

CHAPTER TWO

COLTON GRAVES WAS on the final hour of his shift when Ricky and Jordan pulled up to the gate. A young man in his mid-twenties with a strong jaw and blonde hair cut high and tight, he had moved to the Texas panhandle right out of college when he got the job offer with the Texas Parks and Wildlife Department as a park ranger at Palo Duro Canyon. The public land that made up the northern part of the canyon was a frequent haven for mountain bikers, campers and tourists who wanted to see the famous Lighthouse hoodoo. He enjoyed the work most days, and had been lucky up to this point to not have anyone go missing during his shifts. That was one of his biggest fears, something that would make his heart race at night. He dreaded the call of having to find a missing hiker. Though the canyon was beautiful, and most of the trails were well-maintained and populated, a few wrong turns or a slip down a steep slope could be the difference between a fun excursion and a trip to the emergency room.

He pulled his green Chevy truck into the little dirt lot at the boulder garden trailhead and walked up to the Subaru, shining his flashlight in the windows, searching for any sort of clue or movement. The girl's vehicle, however, was completely empty. The park ranger tried one of the handles, but the door was still locked.

Ricky and Jordan stepped out of their vehicle and walked up to the Subaru as well. "Her backpack isn't in here," Ricky said. "She never came back to the car."

A slip of paper was tucked on the dashboard beneath the windshield and the park ranger shined his flashlight onto it. "I remember this one coming through. Her gate entrance was at three twenty this afternoon," he said, reading from the entry ticket.

"Sounds about right to me, sir," Ricky said. "She left the campus right before three."

"You don't have to call me, sir," Colton said. "You can just call me Colton."

Jordan went to the trailhead, the wide patch of dirt that led off into the brush. The trail led up into the canyon elevation, through a maze of large boulders, some as tall as twenty feet, and to the canyon's edge. However, one could take a fork off the main trail and pass through an opening into the private land that hugged the canyon and to a collection of caves. Cupping her hands around her mouth, she yelled out Rachel's name, her voice shrill and echoing.

The sound of Jordan's voice shouting in the night startled Ricky. He didn't want to believe that Rachel was missing. *Not missing*, he thought. *Just not where she's supposed to be.* That did little to ease his racing mind. Both his brain and his heart were going a million miles an hour as they searched the immediate area of the trailhead for any sign of his sister.

"I'm going to go ahead and call in backup and get some lamps out here to light up the trail," Colton said. "I've got some flashlights in the truck. We can go onto the trail a little, but we shouldn't venture too far off. Plus," his voice drifted. "Well, we just need to stick together."

Ricky and Jordan stood at the front of the trailhead, staring at the dark path in front of them. The hiking trail was dirt, packed from years and years of hikers and tourists and lined with wild brush and mesquite bushes, their little thorns just begging to snag on your clothing.

Colton came up behind them and handed each of them a flashlight. The metal barrel felt heavy in Ricky's hand but the beam was strong, illuminating the path ahead of them for several yards.

"Backup is coming down from the office at the north side, but in the meantime, let's go down the trail a little, see if we find her. She may have fallen and broken an ankle. The boulder garden trail gets pretty steep after about a mile," Colton said.

Jordan took a flashlight as well and let Colton lead them down the trail. They continuously yelled out Rachel's name. Ricky felt a chill on his skin and wished he'd worn something heavier than a t-shirt and a hoodie.

Almost reading his mind, Colton said, "It's going to get colder the later it gets but it won't get below fifty tonight. That's what Doppler Dan from channel five says, anyway."

"How long have you worked here?" Jordan asked.

"About two years. Fresh out of college myself," Colton replied.

"Did you go to WT as well?" she said.

The park ranger shook his head. "No ma'am, I went to a little school down south, in San Angelo."

While they conversed, Ricky kept his eye on the trail and swept his flashlight to the brush beside the trail. In the darkness he could make out the silhouette of the boulders along the trail, these towering rocks that had been deposited in the canyon bed millions of years ago.

It reminded him of being young and going camping with their father. Even though it wasn't one of his favorite activities, he cherished the memories now. A part of him felt a tinge of regret too, for not appreciating those times more in the moment. Their father's favorite camping spot was on the shores of Possum Kingdom Lake, a four-hour drive from their home. Sitting around a campfire at night, the cicadas buzzing in the trees above them, the sounds of the lake water tapping against the shore, all of it was still so vivid in his memory.

Ricky wished he could thank his father for all those camping trips, even if he didn't enjoy them at the time.

Rachel, however, reveled in nature, in the dirt, sleeping under the stars in a sleeping bag. She was never bothered by the bugs, the lizards and the strange sounds at night.

As they continued on the trail, the path getting steeper as it wound through the valley and toward the canyon wall, Ricky vowed to himself that, when they found Rachel, he'd shake her. Shake her for being so stupid to come out here alone, especially late in the afternoon. But then he'd embrace her and promise to come out here more often with her, to experience and try to understand what she saw in this place.

In front of him, Jordan tripped over a dip in the dirt and she tumbled over, nearly falling on her face. Before

Ricky even had time to process the girl's tumble, the park ranger swooped beside her and wrapped his arm around her waist to keep the girl from falling to the dirt.

It was the little things like that, the inability to act without hesitation, that kept him from wooing a girl. Ricky figured that, at this point in life, relationships had sailed on by. He was just one of those people who would be single forever.

Jordan looked up at Colton with her mocha brown eyes and gave him an under-breath *thank you*. They continued on, calling out for Rachel. On the radio attached to his hip, static broke all other silence, and then a voice over the speaker, "Graves, come in."

Colton detached the black plastic brick from his belt and held it to his mouth, "This is Graves."

"We're here at the trailhead."

"Alright," Colton said. "We're on the trail about half a mile. Went looking for the girl. We'll turn back and come to you."

"Anything?" the voice on the radio asked.

Colton looked at Ricky and Jordan, his eyes resolute, though he pursed his lips in the way that signed defeat. "Nothing yet."

CHAPTER THREE

BACK AT THE Boulder Garden trailhead, Ricky, Jordan and Colton were met by two more park rangers, one much older who Ricky assumed was the head ranger. The older man had long black hair, streaked with gray, tied in a ponytail peeking out below his ball-cap. The other was young, like Colton Graves, and Hispanic, with short-cropped black hair that was hidden beneath a Texas Parks and Wildlife ballcap. Both wore dark green uniforms with bright yellow reflective vests. They congregated in the headlights of one of the green Chevy pickups, their shadows spilling long onto the brush and dirt trail ahead of them.

Colton shook hands with the older man and introduced him to Jordan and Ricky. "This is my boss, Chet Smallbone. He's the chief park ranger here."

Mr. Smallbone took their hands and said, "Tell me all you know so far about Ms. Hernandez and her visit to the canyon today."

Ricky started, "Rachel's my sister. She came to the tech lab earlier this afternoon, around three o'clock and said she was coming down to the canyon to take pictures of some Indian carvings in some caves. I expected her back by eight o'clock, but she never showed."

Jordan interjected, "She's my roommate. I was supposed to come with her originally, but decided to stay behind to work on a research project."

As she spoke, Ricky could see tears forming in the corners of the girl's eyes.

She continued, "I wish I'd come with her now."

Smallbone shook his head "It's okay, and it's going to *be* okay. The park is generally safe, as long as people stay on the trails. The only time we have real issues is when people stray off the paths and find themselves in a ravine. Most of the time, it's people trying to take pictures on the edge of one of the cliffs. But you think she came to the boulder trail?"

"Yes sir," Ricky said. "She said there are some caves around this trail that have ancient paintings."

"That's a problem," Smallbone pursed his lips and looked at the other rangers. "There are caves back that way, but they're well off the trail and it can get a little dicey. Plus, the caves are on private property. But we'll start the search party." He turned to the younger subordinate that accompanied him. "Jorge, call in to county for a dog, and let's get some floodlights."

The younger officer who had come down with Smallbone nodded and went to the truck to begin gathering the necessary supplies for their search party. Ricky also heard the crackle of the radio and the call in for a search dog.

Smallbone turned back to them, "What is she wearing? What do we need to look for?"

Jordan answered this time, "She's got an orange North Face jacket and jeans. A blue hiking backpack."

Smallbone nodded. "That's good. Bright colors are good. They'll reflect well off the searchlights. And you didn't see anything on the trail?"

Colton spoke up, "No sir. We saw some boot prints on the trail and called out her name, but didn't hear a response. It's a possibility she's much further down the trail than we went."

"Well, if she's in the caves, she may be further back than you'd think," Smallbone said.

Ricky said, "Sir, is my sister..." he trailed off. "Is my sister going to be okay?"

Smallbone nodded and placed a reassuring hand on Ricky's shoulder, giving it a squeeze. "I think so, son. Don't take this lightly, though. The canyon can be dangerous, especially at night. But it sounds like she's pretty knowledgeable and knows her way through here. Did she carry a whistle?"

"Yes sir, she keeps a survival pack in her backpack. She spends a lot of time down here. She's majoring in Native American anthropology," Ricky said.

"She sounds very smart." Smallbone turned again to his subordinates, who were gearing up floodlights and packing their vests with supplies. "Hey, Colton, go ahead and radio in to DPS. If they've already got the chopper in the air, let's see if we can get them to divert it down here to shine a light as well."

"Yes sir, on it," Colton said. As he packed his gear, first aid kit, flashlights and flares, he gave Ricky and Jordan a nod.

"What can we do, sir?" Jordan asked Smallbone.

He turned back to them, "Stay here, with the trucks. If for some reason she comes back to her vehicle, we'll need to call all the crew back." He unhooked the radio from his belt and handed it to her. "It's like a walkie-talkie. Just push the button on the side to talk. Let us know if she comes back."

Jordan took the device from him, the thing weighty in her hand, much heavier than she'd imagined.

With that, the three park rangers, led by Smallbone, started off down the trail, flashlights waving back and forth, illuminating the trees and brush. As he and Jordan sat on the open tailgate of one of the park rangers' pickup trucks, Ricky felt the muscle spasm in his leg, which caused his knee to bounce up and down in a nervous twitch and he put his hand down to stop it.

"It's going to be okay," Jordan said.

"This just really isn't like her, you know?" Ricky said. "Sure she can be scatter-brained, but to be out here like this? I don't think she's just lost track of time or something. I feel like something bad happened."

"She may have just twisted her ankle on the trail or something and can't walk. We only went down a half-mile or so," Jordan said, trying to reassure Ricky. "That trail is at least four miles long, and then another two at least to the caves. She's smart enough to stay put and let the rescue team come to her. They'll find her."

"I appreciate you coming down here with me," Ricky said.

"Why wouldn't I?" In the dim light under the stars, she gave him a smile that made his heart beat faster and also made him melt. Ever since he and Rachel came to school here and he'd met his sister's roommate, the bohemian girl with dark skin and long legs and those black locks of hair that flowed out in every direction, he knew he was in love. Even if he couldn't admit it to either of them, he felt it in his gut. The double-side of that coin, though, was that he also knew that Jordan could never be into him. She was like his sister, always looking for the next adventure, the next thing to grab her attention. Ricky knew, in that pursuit, he was simply overlooked.

"Have you ever been to the caves that she's so interested in?" Ricky asked.

Jordan shook her head. "No, but they're talked about all the time by Dr. Errington. Some explorer with the Coronado expedition wrote about them in his journals, and then some cowboy from before the Goodnight days found them again, but that's been almost a hundred and fifty years ago. Some people think they're an old wives' tale now."

"So how did she know where to go to try to find them?"

"Well, the cave system is pretty well-known, but the specific entrance to the painting cave isn't. Nobody has ever been able to find the entrance to the paintings, but Rachel said she thought she'd found it from an old map that she found in the library," Jordan said.

"I just don't get it," Ricky sighed. "And I definitely don't understand why she thought she could come down here alone."

"Your sister is headstrong," Jordan said. "She wants what she wants, and no one is getting in her way."

"When we were kids, she wanted a treehouse so bad," Ricky said, reminiscing. "Our dad said he'd build one, but he never did. Well, one day, when he was at work—this had to be in the summer, because we were at home in the middle of the day—Rachel went in the backyard and climbed a tree and started hammering some planks she'd found to the branches. She slipped and fell, and hit her chin on one of the branches. She had to get stitches and everything. That's how she got that scar on her chin."

Jordan tried to stifle her laughter. "Yup, that sounds just like her."

This talking and laughter calmed Ricky down and his leg no longer convulsed from nervousness. A part of him, despite the situation, was enjoying this moment with Jordan. He never thought he'd get this much time with her alone.

They sat on the bed of the green park ranger pickup truck and the temperature continued to drop. In the Texas panhandle, unlike in the southern part of the state that Ricky was from, it wasn't uncommon for the temperature to drop twenty to thirty degrees after the sun went down. In the summer, it was great. In the late fall however? Not so much. He noticed Jordan rubbing her arms with her hands, warming them up.

"Do you want my hoodie?" he asked, pointing to the maroon school hoodie he wore.

"No, I'm fine. It's just getting a little chilly out here, just sitting and doing nothing," she said.

A low humming sound reverberated off the canyon walls and Ricky looked up to see a helicopter, flying low, skim the surface of the canyon edge before dipping down into the valley. Its searchlight was on and began sweeping the area around the trail.

"This is crazy," Ricky said as they watched the helicopter hover, sweeping its light over the trail area.

"They don't play around when it comes to this stuff," Jordan said.

"I am going to have to tell my mom eventually what's going on," he said with a sigh.

"I know." Jordan leaned into him and rested her head on his shoulder. "It's going to be okay, though. You know, as terrible as it sounds, it's probably something stupid. I bet she just twisted her ankle and can't get back to the trail from the caves."

Ricky didn't even hear her words. All he felt was her head on his shoulder, filling him with electricity. It subdued his anxiety for a fleeting moment and they watched as the helicopter flew over the canyon valley, the spotlight sweeping back and forth, its rotors breaking the otherwise quiet stillness.

Ricky felt embarrassed, and he'd never admit it. However, sitting here on the truck tailgate with Jordan, he wanted this moment to last for as long as it could.

CHAPTER FOUR

COLTON HIKED THE boulder garden trail with his superior in the lead. Chet Smallbone, a descendent of the Native tribes that once called the canyon home, was one of the longest-serving park rangers at the state park and had many unfortunate stories of missing or lost hikers over the years. Finding a missing hiker as quickly as possible was his main priority when this kind of situation occurred, as he knew from nearly three decades' worth of experience, that the chances of survival dropped the longer it took. They'd done several training exercises in conjunction with local law enforcement—both county and state—but this was the first time Colton had put that practice into motion. He only hoped that they'd find the girl alive and well, perhaps with a busted ankle or twisted knee. The trails and the canyon ridge where the caves resided were steep and it wasn't out of the realm of possibility to slip and fall several meters before a hard crash-landing against a pile of boulders. Sweeping a floodlight through the brush that lined the packed-dirt trail, Colton was tasked to search for clothing or items dropped by the girl. One of the newer trails in the canyon system, an addition that Smallbone lobbied against due to the dangerous terrain the path cut through, butted against the edge of the public land that separated the state park from private ranch lands.

One of the things that Colton couldn't believe when first coming to work at the canyon was that so much of it was still in private hands. So much beauty, history and unknown discoveries were all under control by wealthy ranch owners. Colton wanted the entire canyon system to be public land, whether state or federal. Of course, he understood the importance of ranching here in the Texas panhandle, but at the same time, this place was just too beautiful for a handful of people to cling to. Though it was coming into early autumn now, which, in this part of the country, lasted about two weeks before a blast of polar air would usher in a windy winter, his favorite time of the year was spring, watching all the cacti in bloom and the Indian paintbrush flowers pop up all over the canyon floor. Now, as he scanned the yellowing brush beside the ever-narrowing trail that led through the boulders, he missed those warm blooming cactus days.

As they walked, the trail illuminated only by moonlight and the scanning and sweeping of their flashlights, the park rangers called out the missing girl's name.

"Rachel! Rachel Hernandez!" Colton called out. He'd pause for a heartbeat or two, to listen for a response and then shout her name again. As he swept his flashlight beam across the brush and tall grass along the side of the trail, his counterparts did the same on the other side while Smallbone kept his light to the ground in front of them, looking for boot tracks in the dirt.

"Anything, sir?" Colton asked as they continued hiking. There wasn't much talking among the four men as they kept their ears and eyes focused on their surroundings, hoping to find the missing college student.

"Not yet," Smallbone replied. "I can see her boot tracks leading this way though."

Behind them, Colton heard the helicopter approach from the north. Colton turned to see it hover and dip into the bowels of the canyon, its spotlight beaming down, sweeping the area in slow, wide swaths. The pilot of the aircraft dipped the nose down briefly to salute the park rangers and signify that he saw them. The spotlight lit up the immediate area and Colton could make out the barbed wire fence just ahead of them that separated the state park from private land. The private land, however, was where the caves were. Though technically off-limits to the public, that didn't stop the more hard-headed and stubborn hikers from making their way through the fencing and trekking out to the caves.

As the search and rescue helicopter continued to the south end of the canyon, the park rangers made it to the barbed wire. "I was hoping we'd find her before we reached the barrier," Smallbone said. With one boot, he pushed the lowest string of fencing to the ground and lifted the higher with a leather-gloved hand. One after the other, the two young rangers dipped between the fencing wires, careful not to catch their uniforms on the metal barbs that poked out.

Technically, they weren't supposed to be on the private ranch land either, but Smallbone had a laissez-faire attitude when it came to finding a lost or injured hiker, land divisions be damned. The girl would get a scolding from the head park ranger when they eventually found her, but until then, he would lead his men wherever they needed to go.

Once through the threshold and onto private land, the trail went nearly nonexistent. There was a thin line of dirt worn over time by hikers that trespassed onto this area. Though officially off-limits to the public, the land owner who staked claim over this part of the canyon never enforced his legal right over it to keep out people from hiking to the caves carved into this section of the canyon wall.

Once the park rangers reached the canyon edge, they had to begin climbing the ridge to the caves. As they marched single-file up the switchback human-made trail up the canyon wall, Colton kept his high-powered LED beam flashlight trained to the ground beneath them. He hated to think it, but it was possible and fairly conceivable that the missing girl had lost her footing and fallen down the canyon wall to the ground below. However, there was no sign of crumbled dirt or rocks recently dislodged from the trail.

"Stop," Smallbone commanded, holding up a hand. His men behind him stopped in place, hugging the canyon wall. "Turn back to the base." The two younger rangers turned in place and marched back down to where the ground met the sheer cliff face.

Back down, Smallbone pointed his flashlight at the ground. "Look at the prints," he said.

Colton pointed his light down to the dirt trail, seeing the bootprints and marks in the loose dirt.

Smallbone continued, "The small set are hers, I'm sure. They're fresh, and there's only one set. I've followed them all the way up, and they lead up to the caves. But, look," Smallbone crouched and pointed in the dirt. "She turned back down the canyon wall and came back to the trail."

"Shouldn't we at least go all the way to the caves, sir?" Jorge asked, but Smallbone shook his head.

"We can see her prints, clear as day. I'm not going to risk you boys getting injured as well. It's dangerous, especially in the dark," the head ranger said.

"But sir," Jorge began to protest.

"He said turn back," Colton reiterated, to his boss's approval.

Smallbone led Colton and Jorge back through the brush toward the barbed wire fencing, careful to trace the boot prints in the dirt back. Colton could see it now, the girl's prints in the trail, sometimes overlapping but clearly showing movement toward and away from the caves. If she'd gone to the caves in the private land area it was safe to assume that, given the boot prints, she didn't stay.

But, it was also plausible to assume that she was definitely alone, given the lack of other fresh prints in the trail.

As the park rangers hiked back to the barbed wire, Smallbone held the fence once again as his subordinates cleared through it, but before climbing through, Colton checked the barbs for fabric strands that may have been caught if she'd climbed through haphazardly. Stuck to one of the barbs, Colton could see a few threads, wispy and blowing in the light night breeze.

"Look, sir," he said, pointing it out to Smallbone.

Smallbone leaned in and pushed his glasses up on the bridge of his nose. "Looks like nylon," he said. "Probably from her jacket." The older man pulled his phone from one of the zippered pockets on his hip and snapped a picture of the threads. "Good eye," he said to Colton.

"Too bad we don't know if she got snagged coming out here or going back to the trailhead," Colton said.

"Look at the tracks though," Smallbone said as he stuffed his phone back into his pocket and pointed his own flashlight at the ground. "Going out to the caves, they're evenly spaced. Coming back, though, they're staggered. She was either in a hurry, or injured. It's reasonable to assume then she got snagged coming back."

Back on state park land, the trail widened and the men swept their lights through the brush of the trail. The helicopter above them swept a long circle, its floodlight sweeping through the brush and canyon crevices. Despite the humming above them, Colton's eyes were now fixed to the dirt.

After a hundred yard past the fence, Smallbone held up a hand. "Colton. Jorge. Look at this." Smallbone knelt to the dirt. "Look at the prints here." He traced his finger along the lines of the boot marks. "She clearly went toward the fence, and she clearly came back. But——"

Jorge cut him off. "They end."

"That's impossible," Colton said. He ran the beam of his flashlight along the dirt, ensuring he wasn't seeing things.

"I noticed it coming out, but didn't want to believe it, either," Smallbone said. "But, there's no doubt. The prints coming back this way clearly end right here."

Colton didn't believe it. Perhaps the girl had doubled back for some reason. But, he knew, they'd see more than one set of prints in the dirt. Did she take off into the brush, off the trail? If so, for what reason? If someone else had been out here at the same time, they'd have seen more than just the girl's boot prints. It was possible, though unlikely, she'd been scared off by a mountain lion. They did, after all, still live in this area, though rare.

Or, perhaps, more preposterous than that, was the idea that the young woman simply vanished.

CHAPTER FIVE

RICKY AND JORDAN were still sitting on the open tailgate of the park ranger truck when they saw headlights coming around a bend in the road. Just beyond one of the bridge crossings that were built over the fork of the Red River that runs through the canyon, the lights were joined by the rumbling of several vehicles.

Another pickup truck pulled up to the trailhead, the vehicle's headlights bright and glaring in Ricky's face. He shielded his eyes with the sleeve of his hoodie as the trucks came to a stop, kicking up dirt in the air as they did. Stepping out of one of the trucks, a large man with a beige cowboy hat came up to Ricky and Jordan and extended his hand.

"Sheriff Jones," he introduced himself as his hand

swallowed Ricky's. The star sewn onto the chest of his uniform read *Randall County* in gold. "So y'all have a young woman lost out on the trail?" he asked.

"I don't think she's lost," Ricky said. "She came out here earlier this afternoon and didn't return to campus this evening. We," he nodded to Jordan, "came out to look for her and the rangers are out on the trail now."

The sheriff ran his tongue over the front of his teeth behind his lips, the handlebar mustache that ringed his mouth protruding as he did. "I'm sure Smallbone got you kids all worked into a frenzy, too," he said. "Don't worry. Young thing probably twisted an ankle out there. They'll have her back in no time. People come out here thinking it's going to be easy just because the trails are marked, but this terrain is unforgiving. One misstep and all of a sudden you're down with a twisted ankle or banged up knee and you're two or three miles from the nearest help."

Jordan spoke up now, "You see this all the time?" she asked.

"Oh yeah," the sheriff said. "In fact," he reached for the radio on his belt, "let's call up to the chopper in the air, ask what they're seeing." He turned the device on and it crackled to life. "Air support, this is Sheriff Jones," he said. "Come in, air."

"DPS Chopper Three here," a voice came through the static. "Good evening, Sheriff. Is that you down at the trailhead?" The searchlight from the helicopter in the air swept across the canyon floor and lit up the trailhead parking area in a bright glow.

"Yes it is. Do you have visual on Smallbone and his men?" the sheriff asked.

"I do. In fact, they're about a hundred yards from you right now," the voice on the radio said.

Ricky and Jordan looked at each other and their eyes lit up. The park rangers were already coming back to them, which must have meant that they found Rachel without much issue.

"They have the girl with them?" the sheriff asked.

"That's a negative, sir," the voice crackled.

Sheriff Jones pursed his lips but he nodded. "I'm sure they're just coming back for a stretcher then."

"A stretcher?" Ricky asked incredulously.

The sheriff flipped off his radio and nodded. "Sure, if she can't walk they'll probably have to carry her out. A stretcher would keep any injuries stabilized. Like I said, happens all the time, kid."

After a few moments, they could hear the shuffling of boots in the dirt as the three park rangers came back to the trailhead. Though Ricky already knew that his sister wasn't with them, he held on to this illogical hope against the fact.

Smallbone came to the pickup where Ricky and Jordan sat and nodded his head to the sheriff. "Skip," he said, tersely.

Sheriff Jones stuck out his hand and Smallbone took it hastily. "Smallbone," the sheriff said. "Been a minute since you've had an issue down here. Things have been going pretty well, I assume."

"They certainly have, Skip."

"Now, let's keep our professionalism here, Smallbone. It's *Sheriff* when we're on duty," Jones said.

Smallbone nodded. "Fine, Sheriff. We need to start a search party, working in expanding perimeters. Can we get a dog from county—Randall or Potter, whichever is faster—and assist?"

"We certainly can, but first, I need to know exactly what we're dealing with," Sheriff Jones said.

Ricky spoke up, "Did you not find my sister? Where's Rachel?"

Smallbone walked over to Ricky and the man put his hand on his shoulder, giving it a paternal squeeze. "Look, son," he said. "We found her prints on the trail, but not her. She may have gotten spooked, maybe a mountain lion ran her off and she went to hide from it. I'm going to do all I can to find your sister, but I need you to stay calm for me, okay?"

Ricky wanted to stay calm. He wanted to maintain his composure and help in any way he could, but the fear and anxiety took over his brain. "What do you mean a *mountain lion*? There are mountain lions out here? Are you saying my sister could have been dragged off by a big ass cat and you don't *know*?"

Smallbone furrowed his brows. "Take a breath, son," he said. "I promise you, we're going to do everything we can to find your sister, but we have to keep our heads."

Ricky was about to lose it, but he felt Jordan's hand slide over on top of his. He looked at her and she gave him a look of reassurance. "They know what they're doing, Ricky," she said. "She's going to be okay."

Feeling his heart thump against his chest, Ricky tried to remain calm, but the sheer fact that the park rangers didn't find her on the trails made his anxiety kick into overdrive. "This is ridiculous," he said. "Surely she didn't just disappear. She's around here somewhere. And you guys are all just standing around!"

Sheriff Jones rolled his eyes. "Someone get this kid a Xanax, good God."

Smallbone turned and shot a perturbed look at the sheriff. "Are you going to get me that dog or not, Skip?"

For a moment, the two men bore down on each other in what Ricky would call a pissing match, but after a beat, the sheriff turned and went back to his truck to make a call into county.

Smallbone turned back to Ricky. "Look, son. If you

can't remain calm, I can't have you out here. There's about to be more men and we're going to mount a search party for your sister, and I want your help. Can you help?"

Ricky's eyes watered but he swallowed and nodded. "Yes, sir."

"And listen," Smallbone said, "the sheriff is a hard ass but as long as you're in my canyon, this is my jurisdiction. We're going to find Rachel."

"I feel like I should call my mom," Ricky said. "To let her know what's going on."

"Where does your mother live, son?" Smallbone asked.

"Decker," Ricky answered. "We're from Decker."

"I'd hold off for now," Smallbone said. "If she were local, I'd have you call her before one of those reporters from channel ten or five caught wind of what's going on down here. I'd hate for her to learn about it over the ten o'clock news. But, no need to alarm anyone right now. It's your call, of course, but that's just my advice, whatever buffalo nickel it's worth."

Ricky pondered the ranger's words for a moment and decided the man was right. Besides, what could their mother do all the way in Decker other than worry? It was at least a six-hour drive from their small hometown to the university, and another thirty minutes to the canyon itself. Ricky decided it would be best to keep mum until the park rangers and search party found her. Worst case scenario she was seriously injured.

No, he thought to himself. *Worst case scenario is she's dead.*

Ricky tossed the thought from his mind. He looked at Jordan who gave him a smile. "He's right," she said. "You'd just keep her up all night, and maybe for no reason."

Ricky gripped the tailgate he and Jordan sat on and felt the cold metal on his hands. It radiated through his body and calmed him. Looking up at the park ranger, he said, "Okay."

"Good," he said. "Now, we've got some more guys coming in from Randall County." He turned and called out to Sheriff Jones, "Where are we on that search dog?"

"Coming down the switchbacks now," the sheriff called back. "Five minutes."

Smallbone nodded and turned back to Ricky, "We're going to mount a search party in this vicinity and work out way outward, basically in an expanding circle away from the trail." As the park ranger spoke, he moved his hands, forming a ball with his fists enclosed and moving them away from each other. "It's very hard to get out of the canyon, and I don't think she's far off."

Jordan spoke up, "Where do you think she went?"

"Honestly?" Smallbone rubbed the back of his neck with one palm. "I think she went off trail and tripped, broke an ankle. She's out there. We just have to go to her. Luckily, it sounds like she's one of the smart ones. If she's injured, she'll know to stay put."

"So how can we help?" Jordan asked.

"Once the rest of the men get here from county, I'll post you up with Ranger Graves. You three will be responsible for a quadrant away from where we found her tracks to veer off."

"Sounds good to me," Ricky said. But as the park ranger walked off to begin discussing the plan with his men, Ricky couldn't help but notice how the sweat beaded on the older man's forehead, how he dabbed at the back of his neck nervously. The man was not as confident as he tried to project.

And, like it or not, Ricky knew something was really, really wrong.

CHAPTER SIX

AFTER ABOUT AN hour, over a dozen men from various local law enforcement agencies propagated at the Boulder Garden trailhead. A black Labrador retriever with an escort from Randall County walked around in the dirt, sniffing the ground. Once all the men had their equipment gathered and slapped a few handshakes amongst themselves, Smallbone stepped to the front of the trail.

"Alright, let's cut to the chase," he said. "We've got a young woman, nineteen years of age, Hispanic. Rachel Hernandez. Came out to the canyon at three this afternoon and didn't show back up at the university this evening. Ranger Graves, Ranger Gomez and I found what we believe are her boot prints on the trail.

We'll start here with the dog. Ranger Graves will lead a party east of the trail. I will take a crew west. Sheriff Jones will lead some of you onto the private land just beyond the fence area. The chopper in the air will provide aerial support. If you find her, radio in coordinates so that the chopper can flood the area. Got it?"

"Sir," Colton Graves spoke up, "shouldn't the park rangers lead the crew to the caves?"

Smallbone raised his eyebrows. "I think it will be fine if the sheriff and his men go. We, after all, have no jurisdiction on private land."

Colton nodded, silent. Sheriff Jones huffed his agreement.

All the men nodded their understanding and they began to march down the trail in the darkness. As they began walking, more vehicles pulled into the parking area, already congested, and Graves groaned as he walked next to Ricky and Jordan. "The vultures are here," he said.

Ricky looked to see two white news station vans. From the passenger seats of each, almost in unison, two attractive young women popped out of the vehicles, straightening their skirts.

Walking past them on the trail and back toward the parking area, Smallbone said, "I'll handle them. Gomez will take my lead." Graves nodded with a, "yes sir," and he continued to usher Ricky and Jordan down the trail.

Ahead of them, the search dog sniffed at the trail and the men followed. After nearly two miles of hiking, the trail climbing up the field of boulders that populated the canyon floor, the dog stopped and pointed with one paw.

Gomez called out, "This is where her prints double back from the caves," he said.

"We'll take the brush to the east from here, then," Graves said as he motioned to Ricky and Jordan.

"Okay, we'll go that way," Jorge pointed west, "while the sheriff takes a crew toward the caves." Jorge then addressed the entire cadre, all dozen of them. "We're on channel two if you see anything," he said.

All the men in the search party nodded and Colton lead the two college students into the brush. Off the trail and away from the group of men with their flashlights illuminating the trail, the canyon got dark quickly and the three of them used their own lights to scan the brush while calling out for Rachel.

His first search and rescue mission since joining the park ranger service, Colton racked his brain for every bit of training he'd had, remembering to call out for Rachel and then to stop to listen for a response. As he examined the ground with his light, he looked for anything that could indicate recent human presence— even something as miniscule as a few strands of polyester threads caught on a mesquite thorn.

"I don't think she would have come off the trail," Ricky said as he swept his flashlight along the ground.

"You'd be surprised what happens when people get scared. They make decisions that, though later they know are irrational, make complete sense in a panic," Colton said.

"Have you done a lot of these search party things?" Jordan asked.

Colton sighed. "No, in fact, this is my first." He turned to her. "But, Smallbone keeps us trained and ready for this kind of situation. We just have to remember that the canyon is wide open, but also pretty enclosed. It's hard to scale the walls, for instance, without equipment. We'll find Rachel."

With her attention on him as he spoke, Jordan tripped on a mesquite brush and nearly fell face-first into the thorns. Colton wrapped his arms around her and pulled her away from it in a flash of reflexes and training.

"You alright?" he asked as he helped her back up to her feet. Ricky came to her side as well and held his light on her legs to make sure she didn't snag on the bush.

She looked up at Colton, her dark brown eyes looking nearly black in the dim light, but she gave him a smile. "Yes, I'm okay." With Colton's help, she got back up to her feet and dusted herself off.

"Got to watch your step," Colton said. "They're not normally out at night, but you wouldn't believe how often people nearly step on a rattlesnake out here."

Ricky looked down at the ground with his flashlight. "Rattlesnakes?" His voice cracked with nervousness. "What if she got bit by a rattlesnake?"

"It's not out of the realm of possibility, but I think we would have found her on the trail," Colton said. "She wouldn't have wandered off with a snake bite. Her leg would swell up and it would be almost impossible to walk."

As they talked, Jordan broke the rattlesnake talk with an excited, "Guys, look at this!"

Colton and Ricky both went over to where she had her flashlight aimed. On the branch of another mesquite brush, a few strands of orange fiber whipped in the air. "You said she wore an orange North Face jacket?"

"Yeah," Ricky said, staring at the threads. They were barely noticeable, but with the light reflecting off them. "Are these new? Can you tell?"

"I would say recent," Colton said. He took out his notebook from the chest pocket of his green field jacket and wrote down the coordinates from his phone. From one of the pouches on his hip, he took out a long strip of reflective plastic and tied it around the branch of the bush.

"Do you hear that?" Ricky asked.

Now that they weren't calling out for Rachel or discussing the dangers of the canyon, Colton cocked his ear to the sound. It was a slow rustle, almost like static in the cool night air.

The three of them walked toward the sound, and just a few yards ahead of them, the brush opened up to a stream of water cutting through the grass. Colton guessed this part of the river was twenty feet wide, and though not very deep—perhaps no more than four feet—it rushed along with a force strong enough to sweep a person downstream.

Colton looked back at the strands of fabric on the bushes, his tie marker floating in the wind, reflecting off his flashlight beam.

"Does this stream go all the way to the caves?" Ricky asked.

Colton nodded. "Close to them, at least."

Ricky broke their silence, "Do you think she…" he trailed off.

"I don't think so," Colton answered. Which really wasn't the truth. It was reasonable to think that the girl had, in a panic, fallen into the river, perhaps injured, and was carried by the current.

Colton stepped away from the two college students and pulled his radio from his belt. "Smallbone, this is Graves, come in."

After a heartbeat of static, his boss came through the speaker. "Go ahead."

"Sir, we're on the eastern edge of the trail. I think we need to get county to bring in a dive team."

Looking back at the two college students that accompanied him, the girl with tears in her eyes, Colton was certain he could actually see their hearts breaking.

CHAPTER SEVEN

RICKY STARED AT the stream just in front of them and, without even thinking, started to jump into the water. His mind went completely blank except for one thought: *She's in there*. It made sense to him—his sister had been spooked off the trail, maybe by one of those snakes that Colton had told them about, and, in the dark, ran in a panic where she'd fallen into the stream. She'd hit her head, perhaps, and was carried by the current to god-knows-where. All senses left him as he sprinted toward the gurgling stream.

He felt the tension on the collar of his hoodie as Colton grabbed ahold of him at the last second. "Whoa, whoa," the park ranger said. "Careful, man."

"She's in there!" Ricky screamed. "We have to save

her!"

"You'll drown in that water," Colton said. "It doesn't look like much, but if it swept you off your feet, the current would pull you under."

Struggling at first against the park ranger's grip, Ricky finally eased up. All the emotion, all the uneasiness erupted to the surface and he burst into tears, immediately embarrassed but unable to stop them from streaking down his face.

Jordan came up next to him and put her hand on his shoulder. "I know this is rough, but it's okay. We don't know that she fell in the water."

"She's right, man," Colton said. "We're going to bring a dive team in to drag the waters, but for now, we need to look for more clues in this area and tag them."

Ricky's tears dried up, though his chest occasionally heaved a heavy, broken breath. It was all so overwhelming, and beyond that, it was completely dark aside from their flashlights. He imagined that he wouldn't feel nearly as unnerved if there was still some daylight, but the smartwatch on his wrist pushed close to eleven o'clock, the Mickey Mouse hands on the square LCD screen both nearly pointing directly up.

At the edge of the river, Colton shined his light to the bank. "If it makes you feel better, I don't see any skid marks in the mud. Unless she actually *jumped* into the water, we'd see her boot marks in the mud going down into the river. I still want to get the dive team in," he said, turning back to Ricky and Jordan, "but I'd be surprised to find her in there."

"Could she have fallen into the water and climbed to the other bank?" Ricky asked.

"That's a good possibility as well," Colton said.

Ricky went to the water's edge and shined his flashlight all along the banks of the river, seeing nothing—at least from what he could tell—out of the ordinary. Or, nothing that screamed at him, *she fell in!* Behind him, Colton continued investigating the brush where they'd found the polyester fibers on the mesquite bush, looking for more. Shining his flashlight down at the ground, Ricky looked for disturbances in the soil, the tell-tale evidence of dirt kicked up from running boots.

The radio on Colton's hip crackled to life, "Graves, this is Smallbone. We've got the dive team from Potter County en route," the head ranger said. "Why don't y'all come back to the trailhead."

Colton spoke into the radio, affirming that they'd received the orders and then motioned to Ricky and Jordan. "They'll take it from here. We've got the coordinates and the area tagged."

The three of them hiked back through the brush and to the trail and made their way to the parking area.

As they got closer to the road, Ricky could see the glow of several vehicles at the trailhead. Lights mounted to the tops of trucks and vans illuminated the area, and as they arrived, he saw nearly a dozen different vehicles, from Jordan's Toyota and his sister's Subaru, which had an evidence tag on the door and the residue of fingerprint dust on the door handle, to the park rangers' pickups and several county law enforcement SUVs. A few yards away, the television vans were parked and idling, dishes mounted on poles on their roofs. The hum of gasoline generators pounded in the night air.

What had started as just he and Jordan coming down to find his sister had turned into an entire operation. He felt simultaneously glad and uneasy. Glad that so many people were looking for her, so many different organizations coming together to dredge the canyon and find his sister. But uneasy that, even with all this, they'd still come up empty-handed.

Smallbone came up to them. "You found something?" he asked Colton.

"Yes, sir," Colton answered. "We found some threads on a bush near the river bank, probably a hundred yards from where her tracks double back off the trail. What I think may have happened is she got ran off—by what, I'm not sure—and in the darkness, fell into the water. I tagged the mesquite with a tie."

Smallbone chewed on this for a moment. "Makes

sense to me. Can you take some of these forensics guys out that way?"

"Absolutely," Colton said as he turned to gather some of the county officers that had congregated at the trailhead.

Ricky felt completely helpless, not knowing what to do, but wanting to do *something.* "Where do you need us, sir?" he asked.

"Honestly, guys, there's not much else you can do. And because we haven't found her, it may be a good idea to give your mother that phone call. With these vultures out here, she's bound to see it on the morning news. I'd hate for her to find out that way." Smallbone said. He paused for a moment and then turned to Jordan, "Are you under the tutelage of Amelia Errington in the anthropology department?"

Jordan said, "Yes, sir. She's our advisor, both mine and Rachel's."

Smallbone nodded and pulled out a khaki-colored field notebook from his back pocket and wrote down a few words. "I'm going to give her a call. Hopefully she's not asleep yet. I'll have to drive up to the rim to get cell signal. Why don't you two ride with me?" he asked. "You can give your mom that phone call up there as well."

Ricky nodded and he and Jordan followed the park ranger to his pickup truck. The interior of the vehicle was dusty and Smallbone wiped the passenger seat clean as best he could to allow Jordan to sit while Ricky took the back bench seat. He squeezed in next to the park ranger's equipment, including some shovels that were still caked with dry mud.

"Sorry about the seats, guys. It's a dirty job sometimes, and this is my mobile office," Smallbone said, though both Ricky and Jordan mumbled courteous *it's fine*'s. Ricky shifted in the seat, feeling dirt clumps on his rear end as they drove away from the Boulder Garden trailhead and toward the state park entrance.

"How long have you been a park ranger, Mr. Smallbone?" Jordan asked.

"This is my twenty-eighth year in the canyon. I started back in the nineties," he answered, keeping his eyes on the dark, winding road, lit only by the headlights of the pickup.

"I can't imagine doing a job that long," she said.

"It's been a fun job, all in all. We have things like this happen from time to time, and that can be scary, but it's few and far between. Most of the time, I get to come to work every day and spend time in nature. I feel like it connects me to my ancestors. Who else gets paid to be outside and enjoy a place like this?" he said.

Ricky sat silent in the backseat, watching the branches of the trees next to the road nearly scrape the sides of the truck. "Do you think someone could have taken her out of the canyon?" he asked, interrupting the conversation going on in the front of the vehicle.

Smallbone peered through the rearview mirror and met Ricky's eyes. "It crossed my mind, of course, but the evidence isn't there. There weren't multiple prints in the dirt, there weren't vehicle tracks other than hers and yours at the trailhead. Even if she was snatched from the trail, we would have seen some kind of evidence of a struggle. Broken branches, feet dragging on the ground. And we didn't see anything like that."

"My sister didn't just *disappear* though, Mr. Smallbone." Ricky said, a hint of indignation in his voice. "People don't vanish. Something happened to her."

"I agree, but I don't think anything nefarious is going on. The canyon is a big place. She could have gotten turned around in the dark. If she went to those caves, there's a chance Amelia—Dr. Errington, I'm sorry—knows some more information about why Rachel went down there, or where she could have ended up." The disbelief must have been thick on Ricky's face because the park ranger said, "It's going to be okay, son. I know you're worried. But you've got the best people for the job down here and they're not going to stop working until we find her."

Smallbone drove the pickup truck up the winding road that hugged the canyon wall and out of the hole.

Up here, the night sky was massive, the glowing star-field above them stretching for as far as Ricky could see.

A convoy of pickups and vans approached them on the road and slowed down as they passed their pickup. The vehicles had emblems on the sides that read *Potter County Sheriff Department*.

"That's the dive team," Smallbone said.

Ricky didn't want to think about the dive team. He didn't want to think about them being necessary. Instead, he pulled his phone from his back pocket, the cell signal bars showing full strength. As the device regained signal, notifications began popping on the screen, mostly emails. He wanted, more than anything, for one of those notifications to be from Rachel. A text asking him *Where are you?* There was nothing, though.

Opening the phone app, he called his mother. The phone rang a couple of times as he held the device to his face. She answered, slightly sleepy.

"Hello?" she said.

"Mom," Ricky said, "I, um." It took him a moment to collect his thoughts. "I just wanted you to know that you're probably going to see on the news in the morning that Rachel is missing."

CHAPTER EIGHT

COLTON MET THE dive team at the trailhead as they pulled up and began unpacking their gear. The leader of the team met him with a hearty handshake.

"You in charge here?" the man whose patch on his jacket read *SMITH* said. He was tall, towering over the rest of them by a good six inches, though lanky with limbs that were toned with muscle. His dark hair was cropped short in a buzz cut.

"I am at the moment. Smallbone is the head park ranger. He went up to the rim to make a call, but he left me for the time being," Colton said.

"Alright, well, tell me what we're looking at here," Smith said succinctly.

Colton gave him the details just as concise. "Missing girl, came out here alone earlier this evening. Her tracks go off toward the caves and then come back but then vanish off the trail about a mile and a half down. We think she ran off into the brush toward the river. Found some strands of fabric on a mesquite bush that match the color and material of her clothing."

Smith nodded, "So you think she fell into the river?"

"It's a possibility, but I think we should weigh and explore every option," Colton answered. "Didn't see any boot tracks leading to the banks."

Despite the evidence found, the girl's boot marks in the dirt, heading toward the caves before circling back and then stopping in the middle of the boulder garden trail, despite the threads of wispy polyester floating in the canyon night air, something ate at the back of Colton's brain. Something that he couldn't quite calculate or form to a complete thought. Perhaps it was the way the girl's tracks just stopped, without turning. None of the brush or limbs of the mesquite off the trail were broken or damaged. No sign of struggle or of the girl wounded. For all he knew, the girl was walking on the trail and then just...vanished.

"She could have tried to jump over the stream and miscalculated the distance," Smith said as he and his crew of four unloaded their equipment to haul to the riverbank. Once they had everything, their snorkels, wetsuits and tags, Colton led them down the trail to the place where the girl's prints doubled back. They were careful not to walk on the trail itself, instead keeping to the edges in order to preserve the evidence of where the young woman had trekked earlier that day.

Yesterday. Colton, looking at the Timex on his wrist saw that the hands had crossed midnight. The exhaustion hit him with the realization that they'd crossed into the next day; what he had hoped was a quick rescue mission, dragging a girl with a broken ankle off the trail with a few painkillers and a field splint had turned into something much more involved and much more intense.

And, he knew their night was only beginning. They'd be out here all night, unless by some miracle the college student showed up.

He dared not think the alternative.

The four men that made up the dive team congregated at the river's edge, scanning the banks for signs of entry by the missing girl, any evidence of her slipping in the mud and into the water. They traced a path from the tag that Colton had left on the mesquite bush where they'd found the threads of fabric. Then, two of the men, fully equipped in wetsuits, flippers and gloves illuminated their waterproof headlamps and waded into the water, which came up to their chests. They gave a salute to their chief at the bank and dipped under the water. Colton watched as they slowly crept along the banks, sweeping from side to side, their heads under the surface, placing their hands on every inch of the dirt and rocks in the riverbed.

As the frogmen worked each bank, moving back to the center in zipper-like movements, the two men hugging the dry land on the bank tagged every few meters with stakes in the ground to signify that the portion of the river had been cleared. Once a portion of the water was cleared, they moved a set of floodlights about ten meters down, working like this slowly and methodically. They moved downstream, working with the flow of the river.

Colton could do nothing but observe the investigation. Then, one of the divers popped out of the water and ripped his mask off.

"I think we have something," he said.

Colton jogged over to the bank and shone his flashlight down on the diver. The frogman held up a clump of orange fabric from the riverbed.

The jacket had been ripped to shreds.

CHAPTER NINE

DOCTOR AMELIA ERRINGTON, Ph.D. arrived at the front entrance of the state park in less than half an hour after Ranger Smallbone had called her and informed her of Rachel's disappearance earlier that evening. The woman had pulled her graying hair into a messy bun tied to the top of her head and her oversized sweater fell to mid-thigh on her tiny frame. Parking her car in one of the vacant spots near the gate, she stomped over to Smallbone's truck where he, Ricky and Jordan waited for her. Smallbone stepped out of the pickup first to greet the woman.

"Alright, what's going on here, Chet?" she asked, exasperated. Seeing Jordan as she stepped out of the pickup, the woman lit up and whatever frustrations she held at seeing the park ranger at this time of night immediately vanished.

"Miss Harris, I certainly didn't expect to see you out here," the woman said.

"Yes ma'am," Jordan said. "We didn't expect to need to call you, either."

Ricky, coming to Jordan's side, introduced himself to the anthropology professor and his sister's advisor. Explaining that Rachel had come out earlier in the day and never returned to campus, the professor seemed more flabbergasted than any of them.

"Those caves, the paintings, that's all legend," Dr. Errington said. "Even if they did exist at one time, they haven't been seen by a verified source in nearly five hundred years."

"Rachel was convinced that she'd found them, though," Ricky said.

"That's," Errington paused, "impossible."

"We were hoping you could give us some information about the kind of things you're teaching your classes," Smallbone said. "We found her prints on one of the trails, but we need you to explain why she would have come down here looking for them."

"I was in the tech lab when she was telling me what she was looking for—the cave paintings. What are they?" Ricky asked.

Smallbone motioned to the truck, still idling, exhaust pouring into the night air in a quickly-disappearing fog. "How about you give us a history lesson on the way down to the trail?" he said.

Smallbone drove them back down into the canyon while Ricky watched the bars of service on his cellphone dwindle down to nothing. The screen then read the dreaded words *No Signal*.

His mother, on the phone call he had with her, had been immediately ballistic, though he calmed her down after a few minutes. She said she'd drive immediately from Decker, though Ricky reminded her there wasn't much they could do except be in the way of the professionals on scene. After a brief argument, she eventually capitulated. He hated waking her with this kind of news, but figured Smallbone was right; it was much better to know now instead of in the morning.

Dr. Errington, riding in the front seat beside Smallbone, spoke as if she were giving a class lecture. "In the pre-Columbian days of the Texas panhandle, there were many Native tribes warring over this piece of land. They warred over control of the river, the bison herds that congregated near it, and the natural shelter the canyon provided. We think of Native Americans as mostly hunter-gatherers, but once a tribe controlled the area, they generally stayed put. The canyon's resources were valuable, and there were many natural fortresses and caves. The cave system Rachel was looking for has been a subject of debate for centuries."

"She showed me a map," Ricky said.

"Me too," Jordan nodded. "She found some hand-drawn maps in the library."

"One of the priests in Coronado's expedition wrote about a great cave full of paintings of magical and mystical properties. He described it in such detail," Errington said. "Hundreds of years later, a cowboy who was herding cattle through the area found it again, by accident. But, despite taking some of his men to the place to show them, he was never able to find it again. It's been kind of an old wives' tale ever since, this magic, mystery cave. I've spent the last few decades myself trying to prove its existence."

"Well, Rachel thought she'd found it," Ricky said. "She was so sure of it."

"If she had, it would be an amazing discovery," Errington said. "No one has seen those cave paintings in half a millennium."

As they discussed Rachel's exploration, Smallbone stopped the truck at the trailhead and they all spilled out of it. There were still several sheriff's deputies in the parking lot. Seeing the newcomer Dr. Errington, one of the blonde reporters stationed next to a white news van came over, a microphone in hand and a large man lugging a camera behind her.

"Excuse me, ma'am," the reporter asked. "Can we ask you a couple of questions?"

Smallbone waved the young woman off, however, "No questions right now, Miss. We're just conducting a routine search operation for a young woman who went off the trail."

The park ranger herded the three of them away from the news reporter who stood in the road, dejected.

"I can answer for myself, Chet," Dr. Errington said under her breath.

"I know you can, Amelia. But right now we don't have time," Smallbone retorted.

He led them down the trail, careful to stay on the sides without walking in the middle, where some investigators were measuring, photographing and tagging the boot prints that were assumedly Rachel's.

"Did she go all the way to the cave?" Dr. Errington asked.

"We believe so, but the curious problem lies on the trail itself," Smallbone said.

They hiked the trail for nearly an hour, the hustle and bustle of the investigation all around them. Several of the investigators and search party members cleared the trail for them.

Finally, they came to an area in the trail that housed multiple floodlights, the generators powering them humming along in the still, cold night.

"What is this?" Dr. Errington asked.

"Look at the prints in the dirt," Smallbone said. "You can see that she clearly went to the cave system and then doubled back, but then…" the park ranger trailed off.

Dr. Errington knelt in the dirt. "They just vanish."

"What I want to know," he said, crossing his arms at his chest, "is what kind of hogwash are you teaching in your class that would compel a young woman to come down here completely alone to search for some cave?"

The professor stood up from her crouch in the dirt, anger immediately streaked across her face.

"How dare you even *suggest*—" she started.

"Spare me, Amelia. I know how much you enjoy proliferating the myths of this canyon to get these kids to take your classes. You teach as much myth as you do actual history."

"You're such a damn fool, Chet. I see you haven't changed one bit," she shook her finger in the man's face, though he had nearly two feet of height on her.

"Neither have you, apparently," he retorted.

"Well, I need to be able to see it, the cave I mean," Dr. Errington said. "If that's where she was going, I need to see what she found."

"That's not going to be possible, Amelia. They're

on private land, and the investigation there is now under the jurisdiction of Sheriff Jones." Smallbone pressed his lips into a line. "You *know* that."

During this bickering, with Ricky and Jordan staring on in collective shock and humor, Colton Graves approached from the brush.

"Graves," Smallbone said, collecting himself. "Any news?"

"Actually, sir…" his voice, shaky, trailed off. He collected himself, "Sheriff Jones is down with the dive team now," he said. "I think you're going to want to come down to the river with me."

Ricky stepped between the park rangers. "Tell me, right now," he demanded of Colton. "Do you think she fell in the river? Do you think she drowned?"

Colton looked up at Smallbone, as if to get permission to speak freely, and then at Ricky. His chin trembled when he spoke. "I'm not going to lie to you, Ricky. They found an orange jacket, the type that you said she wore." He sighed. "It's ripped to shreds. You need to prepare for the worst here."

PALO DURO: A THRILLER

PART TWO

FOUR MONTHS LATER

PALO DURO: A THRILLER

CHAPTER TEN

IT FELT LIKE a missing limb. Missing an entire part of your being, and even if he tried to continue on, living his normal life, Ricky couldn't help but wake up every morning feeling like part of him was no longer there. He'd gone through the stages of grief, but he couldn't quite get to the *acceptance*, acknowledging that his twin sister, the one person in the world who seemed to "get him" was gone.

More than anything, he hated *not knowing*. He waited every single day for some breaking news from one of the local television stations, some sheriff's deputy—or even Colton Graves—to call him, to come to his dorm, to request a meeting. And tell him the thing he both dreaded and wished for.

That they'd found her body.

But, that would mean it would be over and he could finally move on. He wanted closure. He wanted to finally know what happened to Rachel that night in that godforsaken hole in the ground.

It was strange to have your worst nightmare be also the thing you wanted the most.

He stayed enrolled in school, because that's what Rachel would want. His grades weren't what they once were. Half-finished projects remained in pieces on his desk in his dorm room. His mother begged him over Christmas break to stay in Decker, and a part of him felt guilty for not listening to her.

She was alone as well.

But he couldn't stay there. He wanted to be back here on this campus, not necessarily for the education, but to be the first one to know if some development occurred. He wanted to be *here*.

Those news stations, though, seemed to have completely forgotten about the story of the young woman missing in the canyon. Rachel's name popped up on the news more and more infrequently as newer and more exigent things took up the airwaves.

Things were changing all around campus. It was starting to get warmer in the mornings, and as he walked to the computer lab under the blossoming trees on the university grounds, black headphones covering his ears and the sounds of The Maine drowning out all other noise, Ricky wasn't even paying attention to the girl calling out his name.

He felt the tap on his shoulder, and he pulled off the headphones and turned to see her standing in front of him.

"Oh. Hey Jordan," he said.

"Hey, I saw you walking and I just wanted to come over and ask how you were doing. I haven't talked to you since we got back from Christmas break. Are you okay?" She wore a maroon hoodie, much like the one she wore to the canyon that night. He'd had such a crush on her, fumbling every time he was around her. Now, it was hard to look at her.

"Um," Ricky said, collecting himself. "Yeah, I'm fine."

"That's good. Are you going back home for Spring Break?" she asked.

Ricky continued walking and she stayed in lockstep with him. "Yeah, probably."

"Okay," she said. "Well, listen, I found a couple of Rachel's shirts in the dorm. If you wanted them, I'm sure your mom would like them back."

Wouldn't Rachel want them to still be there when she comes back? was his first thought. But he quickly shook it from his mind, as well as the indignation. Rachel was gone. The official theory, though they'd never found her body to say conclusively, was that she'd drowned in the river.

"Yeah, that sounds good. I'll let you know for sure," he said. "How's Colton?"

"He's good," she said. "Works a lot, as you know. But things are good. I'm supposed to see him after his shift this evening."

"Right, yeah. Well, I hope everything works out between you two." Ricky pulled the headphones back over his ears and continued his morning walk across campus.

If it weren't for Rachel going missing, Jordan may have never met that park ranger. The night they were looking for his sister, Ricky had felt Jordan's warmth, sitting on the open tailgate of Ranger Chet Smallbone's truck. It was a fleeting moment of something he knew wasn't real, though. There was no way that Jordan could be into him, she the gorgeous and intelligent anthropology student and he the computer nerd.

In a sense, he was happy for her, and for Colton. At least something positive came out of that night.

At the same time, Ricky still had dreams of sitting underneath the stars with Jordan, her head resting on his shoulder as her perfume wafted in the night air. For more than one reason, he wanted to keep dreaming.

Once he got to his statistics class in the classroom center, he took a seat in one of the desks in the back of the lecture hall, which was nothing more than a square room with all white walls except for the line of windows that looked down on the central avenue that ran the length of campus.

He pulled his Lenovo laptop from his bag and powered it on. Most college students, if you asked them what kind of computer they wished for, would tell you they wanted an Apple laptop, one of the sleek aluminum MacBooks. Ricky, however, preferred the Lenovo that he loaded with a version of the Linux operating system called Ubuntu. The free and open-source operating system meant he could compile programs and code machines that a "normal" computer couldn't handle. Plus, he liked being able to customize the look and feel of the interface in any way that he pleased. He had full control over this little machine.

One of the other students, a bulky young man named Ben who wore a cowboy hat most days, tapped Ricky on the shoulder. "Hey man," the student said in his thick Texas drawl. "You're good with this stuff. Can you help me out real quick?" He pointed to his computer.

Ricky twisted in his seat and the young man turned the screen of his laptop so that they could both see. "This program froze up on me, and now all my work got blanked out."

Hitting a couple of keys on the black keyboard,

Ricky brought up the command prompt and ran an explorer program that allowed him to see the cached data left over from unsaved files. He pulled the excel file in the folder over to the desktop, renamed it and clicked it to open it up. The entire file, with all of the cowboy's unsaved data, opened up in a new window.

"Dude," Ben the cowboy said, "how did you do that? You're like a genius. Seriously, I think you're the smartest person at this entire school."

"Eh, it's not that hard actually," Ricky said. "You just have to know where to look."

"Man, for real, you're cool as shit." He held out his fist, inviting Ricky to bump it with his own, which he sheepishly did. "Hey, you need to come hang out with us tonight. The whole crew goes to Boot Scootin' to party the night before a game. Seriously, you should come."

At first, Ricky brushed off the invitation. The last thing he wanted was to be around a bunch of drunk idiots. But at the same time, maybe that's exactly what he needed—a night to completely forget everything and just let loose. Have *fun*. And to completely forget that Jordan would be out with Colton Graves. He couldn't allow himself to stay cooped up in his dorm while they were out on the town.

"Sounds cool. I'll see if I can make it out," Ricky said.

The professor, a short man named Dennis Berry with long strands of white hair that fell down to his shoulders, walked into the lecture hall and plopped his leather briefcase on the wooden desk at the front of the room, his normal routine. "Good morning, y'all," Dr. Berry said. "Hope you got the assignment done. Let's talk about correlation and causation."

Ricky heard the words, but his mind was elsewhere. He thought about the nightclub, Boot Scootin', and the party and all the students that would be there. And, in his mind, he imagined running into Jordan while he danced with another girl, and all of his worries dripped away.

CHAPTER ELEVEN

AFTER HIS TWO morning classes—Intro to Statistics and a Programming Languages course that he had to convince the department head to allow him to take a year early—Ricky walked back into his dorm and tossed his backpack on the ground next to his computer desk. The desk's surface was littered with computer boards and wires. Ricky collapsed face-down on his mattress. Most students that lived on campus in the dorms had a roommate, but Ricky was fortunate that his assigned roommate decided not to live on campus just before school started, and the school hadn't issued the room to anyone else. Before Rachel went missing, though, he rarely spent more than a few hours a day here. Now, if he wasn't in class, he was right here, face down on the twin-sized mattress.

That canyon haunted his thoughts when he was alone like this. All that land out there. Even with the trail and area where they'd found evidence of Rachel roped off and under surveillance, and completely shut off from public access, they still found nothing. *Nothing*. Rachel had up and vanished.

Except, Ricky knew, people don't just vanish. Something happened to her. And without finding any evidence of her actually drowning in that river, he couldn't accept the idea that she'd succumbed to the water. It didn't make sense to him. Rachel was a great swimmer, spending more summers at the lake than anyone else he knew.

As Ricky lay on the bed, going over every bit of information in his brain from the night Rachel went missing, there was a knock on his dorm room door. He ignored it for a moment, being on the verge of sleep when the knocks repeated, this time louder.

"Ricky!" he heard the voice outside the door. Again, a knock and then his name. "Ricky, please open up!"

Peeling himself from the bed, Ricky looked at the clock on his nightstand. The red LCD read just after 6:30. He'd been asleep for nearly four hours. Again, the knocks on the door prompted him to call out, "Alright, give me a second." He shuffled his socked feet over and answered the door.

He knew, even before he'd opened the door that it was Jordan. Ricky's first thought was that she'd brought Rachel's belongings, the hoodies and things that still resided in their dorm. Officially, Rachel was still enrolled in school and was still a student, so Jordan was also not assigned a new roommate. Looking at Jordan standing in the hallway, her face distraught, Ricky sensed something wasn't right.

"Ricky, we need to get down to the canyon," she said breathlessly. "Colton called me. He cancelled our date this evening and now there's a ton of law enforcement down there. He couldn't tell me what they've found, but it has something to do with Rachel."

Ricky was speechless. He stood, propped against the door, his brain still trying to form a coherent thought. The first one—*I was supposed to go to Boot Scootin'*—felt foreign, unwanted. But then, all the emotions flooded in. What had they found, after four months? He didn't want to know.

"Come on," she implored. "Let's get down there!"

He grabbed a gray hoodie hanging from the doorknob of his singular closet and as they ran out of the building toward the student parking lot behind the dorm, Ricky asked, "Are you sure it has to do with Rachel?"

"I'm pretty sure, because he wouldn't give me any

information. But we're going to find out for ourselves," she said.

Ricky pulled the hoodie over his head as they made it to Jordan's Toyota and she fired the vehicle up, tearing out of the parking lot. They headed east, out of town and toward the canyon. The sun crept toward the ground behind them, filling the cab of the car in brilliant orange and pink hues as it began its descent along the horizon line.

"What exactly did Colton say?" he asked.

"Just that he had to cancel our date tonight and they were waiting on some investigators from county to make it out to the canyon. That it might be awhile," she said. "I asked if it had to do with Rachel and he wouldn't answer. He just kept apologizing."

Ricky's heart sank. He wanted to know, yet, as they say, *ignorance is bliss*. If there was some concrete evidence, some testament of Rachel's disappearance, it was no longer this ethereal thing, this open-ended question. If the park rangers found something after four months of searching, four months of open questions, then those questions would finally have answers. And answers meant the end.

As they reached the entrance of the canyon, his heart continued to flutter. A part of him wanted the answers. A part of him was ready for this nightmare to finally be over.

As Jordan drove her car down the winding road that descended into the state park, they heard a buzzing overhead and both looked up to see a helicopter swoop down, its searchlight raking back and forth over the land. Ricky then turned his gaze to Jordan.

"I'm scared," she said.

"Yeah," he said. "I am too."

Even in the fading daylight, Ricky could see the canyon looked different from before. The vegetation and brush were greener, blossoming flowers lined the road. The cacti, little patches of round plants covered in spikes, had little blossoms on top of them. The difference between the drab brown of autumn and the bloom of spring was astounding.

As Jordan drove toward the boulder garden trailhead parking area, they were stopped by a roadblock. Two reflective saw horses were parked in the middle of the road accompanied by a pair of park rangers. Rachel pulled her Toyota in front of the men and stepped out. "Where's Colton?" she asked.

One of the park rangers—Ricky recognized him from the night Rachel disappeared—stepped forward. "I'm sorry, Miss Harris, you can't be down here. This is an official—"

Jordan cut him off. "Jorge. Where *is he*?"

Jorge the park ranger stepped closer to the car. His eyes met Ricky's when he reached the open door.

"Look, Jordan, I can't let you through. This is an official investigation."

"What did you guys find?" Ricky asked. "Can you tell me that?"

Jorge shook his head. "Y'all can't be down here," he reiterated. "Go back to the campus."

"Please," Ricky pleaded. "That's my sister out there."

Jorge didn't budge and Jordan rolled her eyes. "Call Colton," she persisted. "Tell him we're here."

The second park ranger, tall and bearded, his brass nametag reading TOOLEY, stepped forward to back up his partner. "Ma'am, this entire section is closed due to an ongoing investigation. I suggest you—"

Jorge held up a hand to his partner. "She's not going to make trouble," he said. "She knew the girl that went missing. The guy is the victim's brother."

"Yeah, and I'm Colton's girlfriend," Jordan added. The words made Ricky flinch a bit, like hitting the spot on your knee that makes the leg kick. A reflex of disappointment. He knew that they were *together*, but he hated the confirmation of it.

Instead of dwelling on the words, Ricky, one foot in the car as he leaned on the open passenger door, said, "Can you please at least tell us anything? Did they find my sister?"

After a moment, perhaps seeing the desperation in

Ricky's eyes, Jorge came around the car to him. "Look, man. I'm sorry about everything you've been through over the last few months. I know it's been hard, not getting any answers. But, no, we didn't find her."

"Then what is all this for?" Jordan asked, exasperated.

"I can't say. I'm sorry. Now, please, turn around and leave the canyon," Jorge said.

After a momentary stare-down, Jordan said, "Fine. We'll leave." She stepped back into the vehicle and Ricky followed suit.

"Well, this was a waste of time," he said.

"Put your seatbelt on." Her knuckles were white on the steering wheel.

Ricky immediately felt the unease in the pit of his stomach. "What are you doing?" He imagined them barreling through the barrier in the road, running through the roadblock, her car knocking the wooden sawhorses and park rangers to the side of the road as she careened the vehicle toward the boulder garden trailhead. They would be arrested, spending the night in jail.

However, she put her little navy blue Toyota SUV in reverse and pulled away from the barrier.

"Are we leaving? Just like that?" Ricky asked, but she didn't answer.

Instead, Jordan kept her eyes on the road and once

they were around the bend in the road where the park rangers could no longer see her taillights, she pulled over onto the dirt shoulder that hugged the road.

"Get out," she said.

Ricky just stared at her. He wasn't going to be stuck here in the middle of the canyon by himself in the dark. Jordan got out of the car. "Come on," she said.

"What are we doing?" he asked.

"They've got the roads blocked, so we're going to walk through the trails til we find Colton or Smallbone or someone who can give us some answers."

Ricky gulped. This is not what he had in mind for his Friday night. Nonetheless, he acquiesced. Stepping out into the moonlight, into the cacophony of the canyon, he followed Jordan as she started on one of the dirt trails, walking back toward the boulder gardens.

CHAPTER TWELVE

COLTON GRAVES DUCKED under the yellow tape that cordoned off the trail and approached Chet Smallbone. The older man was speaking with the sheriff. "Well, hell no," he heard Smallbone object to a question, "but we don't have eyes on the trail twenty-four-seven either, Sheriff."

"What's going on, sir?" Colton asked.

Smallbone turned to Colton. "Sheriff Jones here is inquiring about our policies on the trails."

"Well, Sheriff," Colton said, "this trail has been off-limits to the public ever since the girl's disappearance, but of course we can't and don't have the manpower to monitor it constantly. Now, I don't know, maybe if we had more state funding, or of course, if you could dispatch a deputy or two, seeing as how we're still in the county—"

"Look here, son," Sheriff Jones cut him off, "all I'm asking is if you or your crew have allowed anyone else on these trails, either this one or the surrounding ones, recently. No need to be a smartass."

Smallbone answered, "No, we haven't. We've had signs and tape up for months. And anyone who's somehow wandered off course, we've politely, yet sternly, reminded them that trespassing on an off-limits area is subject to fine or arrest."

The three men stood under the light of one of the multitude of portable floodlights that had been erected along the boulder garden trail, the power generator humming off in the distance. What they'd found in the brush just off the trail—or, namely, what an errant hiker, off-course, searching for a primitive campground had found—was bewildering, to say the least. That errant hiker also found himself in the back of a deputy's SUV, handcuffed and flummoxed. Though, if Colton had to guess, the guy would be released shortly. He was from out of state, a tourist coming down to the canyon on a vacation trip that had suddenly turned into a not-fun night for him.

There were no tracks in the soft earth leading away from the discovery, and the device that was discovered looked in *too* good condition to have been left there.

No weathering, no real wear on it. It was as if it'd been dropped a few hours ago, not four months.

Behind them, a rustling in the brush off the trail startled the three men congregated on the trail and Colton turned to shine his Maglite flashlight to the sound. The last thing they wanted now was a bobcat making trouble.

"Oh, you've got to be kidding me," Colton said, incensed, as Jordan and Ricky emerged from the darkness. Ricky had his cellphone out, the camera flashlight on to illuminate their way through the dirt.

"I think I stepped through a cactus back there. My leg is on fire," Ricky groaned.

Colton moved his light down to the kid's leg and, sure enough, what looked like six cactus spines stuck out from his ankle.

"What are you doing out here?" Colton asked. He was irate and he could feel his pulse radiating in his ears.

"Coming to find out what the hell is going on," Jordan said. "You can't just leave me on read and not expect me to try to figure out why you won't tell me what you guys found down here. We deserve answers, Colton."

Smallbone and Sheriff Jones looked bewildered at this sudden appearance of the two college kids out of the wilderness.

"We need to get you two off the trail," Colton said. "And, Ricky, you're gonna need some medical attention before that ankle swells up." He turned to his boss and the Sheriff. "Sirs, may I escort these two back to the trailhead?" he asked, gesturing back toward the parking area.

Smallbone waved them off, almost chuckling, but also giving them a look of displeasure.

Once they were out of earshot of the older men, Colton turned to them. "I cannot believe you two. This isn't some campus intramural event where you can do whatever you want. This is an official investigation. The only thing keeping you out of handcuffs in the back of a cop car right now is the fact that we're dating." He pointed his finger in Jordan's face.

Jordan crossed her arms. "We've been waiting for answers for four months, Colton," she said. "You get any sliver of information, and we want to know."

"I don't know why you have to be so damn contumacious," Colton heaved.

"Contu-*what*?" Jordan exploded.

"You can't leave well enough alone! You couldn't wait just a few hours for us to secure this area and figure out exactly what we're dealing with," he said.

Ricky spoke up, "Guys, can we finish this argument at the trailhead so I can get this cactus out of my foot? Please?"

Colton obliged and, putting Ricky's arm over his shoulders, helped the kid limp on the trail toward the parking area where there were several vehicles parked, along with a handful of county officials who all looked confused to see Colton escorting these two college students off a trail that had been roped off hours ago.

"Find some stragglers, Graves?" one of the deputies congregating at the trailhead asked, though Colton waved him off.

"Not quite," Colton said. "This one stepped in a cactus."

The county officials offered their assistance, but Colton politely declined. "He'll be fine, thank you gentlemen," he said.

Colton helped Ricky to the open tailgate of his pickup and as Ricky hoisted himself up, the young park ranger rummaged around in a canvas bag in the truck bed until he found a pair of needle nose pliers.

Kneeling on the ground in the light of one of the generator-powered floodlights, Colton gently removed Ricky's sneaker.

"You should wear more protective footwear out here," he said.

"Well, I didn't have much warning. She came to my dorm and basically dragged me out," Ricky said, nodding to Jordan who stood off to the side with her arms crossed.

"Are you going to tell us what's going on out here or not?" she demanded.

"Look," Colton said, turning to her, "let me get these out of his ankle first, alright?" He turned his attention back to Ricky and, placing the head of the pliers around one of the spines sticking from his ankle said, "This is going to hurt. I'm going to count to three."

Ricky nodded, placing the neck of his hoodie in his mouth and biting down on the fabric.

"Alright. One, two," and before he got to three, Colton yanked on the cactus spine as Ricky screamed between his teeth.

"Jesus *Christ!*" he exclaimed. "You said you were counting to three!"

"I know, it's just easier when I," as he spoke, Colton pulled out another spine and again, Ricky yelled out, attracting the attention of some of the first responders and news journalists in the parking area.

"He's alright," Colton called out, waving them away. "Just stepped on a cactus."

This continued a couple more times, the yank and the yell, until Colton had all the cactus spines, five in total, out of Ricky's leg. From the cab of his pickup, Colton retrieved a bottle of water and a travel-size Tylenol package.

"Take these, it'll help with the swelling," he said, handing the medicine and water to Ricky.

Ricky ripped open the plastic wrapper and, popping the pills in his mouth, chugged the water.

"Okay, *now* tell us," Jordan said.

Ricky looked up. "No, it's okay. I don't want to know." He looked out onto the trail, shadows from the lights above them creating long, weird shadows in the brush on either side of the dirt. "It's been four months. I don't want to know what's left."

The look on the young man's face was one of defeat, of knowing that the answers that he'd get now, after all this time, would be nothing but heartache.

"I understand," Colton said. "Which is why I didn't want you two out here," he glanced at Jordan, who looked down at the dirt, trying to hide her guilt. "But, we only have more questions than answers now."

"What do you mean?" Jordan asked, shuffling some pebbles with the tip of her shoe.

"We still don't have much evidence of what happened to her," he said. "We didn't find a body or anything like that. Still no tracks leading away from the trail."

"So what did you find then?" Ricky asked.

Colton pursed his lips. He contemplated how he should tell them, knowing that the answer would only make them question even more what happened to Rachel Hernandez those four months ago when she up and vanished. He decided that the only answer worth giving was straight, no chaser.

"Her phone," he finally said with a sigh. "We found her phone."

CHAPTER THIRTEEN

"HER PHONE?!" JORDAN shrieked. "Well, that's great, right? That means that she was around here, right?"

"Look guys, I can't give you a whole lot of information more than that. Now keep it down before one of these news girls hears you," Colton said.

Ricky, however, remained speechless. Silently, he cursed this canyon, this godforsaken hole in the ground in the godforsaken flat plains with its godforsaken cactus thorns. If only she'd had cell service, he could have accurately found her location using the device's GPS and signal. Instead, down here, there was no signal and she'd disappeared without leaving behind any way for them to find out what happened. Even now, if they'd found her device, it had been through an entire winter in the elements, the rain and snow and mud rendering the electronic components useless.

Jordan, however, continued her interrogation. "Does it turn on? Did you get any information off of it?"

"Look, I don't know," Colton said. "But there's nothing you two can do down here. Go back home. I'll let you know as soon as I know anything more."

"How did you find it?" Ricky asked, breaking his silence.

"It was in the bushes off the trail. The screen is cracked and it doesn't turn on, which is to be expected. We've got forensics guys over there now, running a bunch of tests," he said.

"How do you know it's hers, then?" Jordan asked. "If it doesn't turn on, it could be anyone's."

"Well, the device matches the description you gave when she went missing. But also," he paused, "her initials are carved on the back."

"Like laser engraving? I don't remember her getting her initials engraved on that," Ricky said.

"No, more like with a rock. Crudely done," Colton said. "So either she did it herself, or someone took her and is now toying with us. But, there aren't any footprints or tracks leading to it on the trail either, so I don't know how long it's been there."

"There wouldn't be any tracks though if it had been there since she went missing," Jordan objected.

By the look on his face, Ricky could see that Colton had already given them more information than he was supposed to. "That's the thing," Colton said. "It looks like it was dropped *recently*."

Ricky's eyes widened as his head popped up. "Wait, so it's not water-damaged? It wasn't in the river?"

"Guys, seriously, I can't say anymore, okay?" Colton held his hands up in protest and gave a concerned look toward the news vans and the media journalists who had taken an interest in their conversation. "Go back home. I promise you, I'll keep you in the loop, but for now, I need to get back to the trail. Where did you park your car?"

Jordan looked at him for a moment, this poker stare-down, but she eventually folded. "Down the road, near the river crossing," she said.

Colton whistled over one of the sheriff's deputies. "These two need to be taken back to their vehicle, about a mile up the road toward the RV campgrounds. Can you escort them?"

The deputy nodded and led the two college students to his SUV, where they climbed in the back, Ricky's ankle still stinging with every step. After a short drive up the road and through the barrier that had blocked their way earlier, they were dropped back off at Jordan's Toyota.

They drove back out of the canyon with not even the radio to drown out the silence between them. As they climbed out of the canyon, their phones, reattaching to their respective networks, began dinging with notifications. Ricky had a message from Ben.

You still down for tonight? He clicked the phone off without responding.

Ricky's ankle still throbbed but the bite of the pain had subsided. The dull ache in his foot matched his heartbeat and his head thumped from the information dump.

And the unknowing. All the new questions.

They pulled into the dormitory parking lot and, limping, Ricky started for his building.

"Hey," Jordan called out, though Ricky kept walking. She ran over and grabbed him by the elbow. "Ricky," she pleaded.

He turned to face her. "I didn't even want to go down there tonight, and you just couldn't leave it alone, let those men do their jobs."

"I want answers!" she screamed in his face.

"I do too!" he screamed back. "But I don't want to see her dead body in that hole in the ground." He collected himself, pulling in three long, full breaths. "I want answers, but at the same time, I don't. Does that make sense?"

She nodded.

"She's still out there, somewhere. I can feel it," he continued. "And it may be stupid, but I believe that. And if the answers we find prove that to be true, I don't know if I can handle it. I want it and I don't. I want the closure and I want to keep believing."

"They found her *phone* though," she said. "That can't be just incidental."

"With her initials carved in the back," he said. "Something really weird is going on, and I honestly don't know if I want the truth."

Jordan pulled him into a hug and his arms instinctively wrapped around her waist. She felt warm against him. Her curly black hair smelled like coconut, sweet and sugary. "I'm sorry," she said into his shoulder.

Her embrace was perfect. In the midst of anger, of the throbbing in his ankle, of the unanswered questions and the chaos, he melted in her embrace. This little bit of peace was perfect.

CHAPTER FOURTEEN

RICKY'S PHONE DINGED again and he picked it up to read the incoming instant message. It was from Ben.

We're pregaming in the parking lot before we head out. You coming?

Ricky thought about it for just a moment, and then decided that, yes, he was.

Sounds good to me, he thumbed out. *Where do I need to go?*

He waited for a few seconds, then little bubbles appearing on his screen. *Come to the south lot. We've got a group waiting by the truck. You won't miss it.*

Ricky figured he could do one of two things tonight: he could sit in this dorm room by himself, waiting for any kind of news, pacing back and forth until he couldn't bear it anymore; or he could go have fun with some of his classmates for once and tuck all this stuff in a cabinet in the back of his brain. He, of course, had forgone all the partying in high school. Rachel had shown up at home well after curfew more than once, however, boozed and buzzed. He never saw the point of it, the tipsy nights that turned into nauseous mornings.

But, hell, he thought. *If there was ever a time to drink, this was it.*

He slipped his sneakers back on his feet, having pulled them off to allow his swollen ankle to breathe. The skin around his foot was still tender and it hurt to walk, but it was much more bearable than it had been just a couple hours earlier. He still couldn't believe that he and Jordan had traipsed through the dark, unprotected brush of the canyon. He knew going in that it was not one of the smartest things they'd done. However, many decisions made in the haste of anger were rarely smart.

On his way out, he checked himself in the mirror on the closet door and tucked his long hair behind his ear. He'd always kept his hair long, wavy black tresses pushed back behind his ears. He'd let it go in the last four months and he was beginning to look, as his mother would say, shaggy.

He walked across campus and there were several pickup trucks parked in the south lot behind the classroom center. Music blared from one vehicle's excessive sound system. The bass thumped and Ricky could feel it hit in his chest as he approached.

"Hey, Ricky!" he heard Ben call out as his classmate approached him with a hand held out. Ricky gave him a high-five.

"Guys," Ben said as he grabbed Ricky by the shoulder and led him to the congregation, "this is literally the smartest kid at this whole school."

Ricky immediately felt out of place. All the guys circled between their vehicles wore cowboy boots and International Harvester hats. They all looked like they belonged on a farm raising chickens and cows, not thumping hip hop music on a Friday night. The guys here nonetheless all greeted him, some with bottom lips full of Copenhagen, and welcomed him into their circle.

Ben pulled a bottle from a large white cooler in the bed of his pickup truck and handed it to Ricky. "Here man, you're gonna need this," he said.

It was a bottle of water.

"Stay hydrated. It'll keep you from getting a hangover," Ben continued.

"Oh, right," Ricky said. "Yeah, I don't want a hangover."

"Hey man," one of the guys said as he slapped Ben on the back, "this son of a bitch right here was so hungover he threw up all over the back of some chick at the Homecoming game. I'm talking *chunks*, man. I'm surprised they even let him back in the stadium that season."

"That's what I get for trying to keep up with you," Ben punched his friend on the shoulder.

"So where are you from, big guy?" the friend asked Ricky.

"Originally from Decker," he answered, taking a gulp from his water bottle. "Down near San Antonio."

"Oh yeah, I know where that is," the kid said. He stuck out his hand. "I'm Brad."

"Ricky." He shook Brad's hand, the kid squeezing hard.

"What brought you up here?" he asked.

"My," Ricky paused. "My sister, actually. We're twins. She chose this school and I followed suit. Mom wanted us to stay together."

"That's cool. Who's your sister?" Brad asked, but before Ricky could answer, Ben pushed him back toward the gathering crowd.

"Don't worry about it, horn-dog. Go get everyone together. Tell them it's time to load up," Ben said.

"Thanks," Ricky said, relieved from having to divulge the story of his missing twin.

"Grab another bottle for the road. You'll thank me later," Ben said. He turned to tell all the guys it was time to head out and Ricky grabbed another bottle of water from the freezing slush of the open cooler in the back of Ben's pickup. He already needed to pee.

* * *

His head was swimming and his stomach felt bloated and, letting out a long, loud belch, Ricky could feel it all coming back up. With little warning, he doubled over a nearby plastic trash can and vomit exploded from his mouth, splashing into the black liner.

"We got a puker!" he heard a voice that sounded both far away and extremely close.

Ricky pulled his head from the maw of the Rubbermaid can, looked at Ben who was laughing his ass off, and doubled over again, hurling warm, acidic liquid from his gullet. The immediate nausea subsided and he felt like he'd be okay.

"Man, I ain't ever seen anyone hurl like that. Holy shit, Ricky," Ben said. "No more beer for you." He laughed and Ricky kind of teetered on his feet. Ben steadied him. "How about we head outside, get some fresh air?"

Ricky nodded and the two of them went out to the patio of the bar. The night air, cool and damp, was a nice change from the warmth and smells inside.

"You lost your p-card on the first night. You gonna make it, chief?" Ben asked as Ricky leaned against the brick of the building.

"Yeah, I think so," he slurred his answer into a semi-comprehensible string of consonants and syllables.

He stared out to the parking lot of Boot Scootin', the sound of country music blaring every time someone opened the door, the haze and stench from inside wafting out. All these vehicles for all these people, mostly college students with fake ID's, all spending their Friday night partying before the big baseball game tomorrow.

"You sure you're okay, bud?"

"They found her phone today," Ricky said.

"What? Whose phone? What are you talking about?" Ben asked.

"My sister. Out in the canyon. The park rangers, the sheriffs. They're all out there, looking for her." Ricky nodded toward the direction of the canyon. Or, at least he assumed it was that direction. He really couldn't tell north from his elbow at the moment.

"Whoa, man," Ben said. "I had no idea. That's crazy. Do they have any clues then? Any leads?"

"No. But it's not like they'd tell us." Ricky's temples were already pounding and every time he turned his head it felt like it took a moment for his vision to catch up. "I'm just so tired of waiting for answers."

"Did you get to see it?"

"The phone?" Ricky asked. "No. By the time we got out there, the park rangers were swarming the place. Wouldn't let us near."

"It's too bad you couldn't look at it, see what she did before she disappeared," Ben said as he tucked a wad of dip between his bottom gum and lip. He stuck the can of Copenhagen in his back pocket and wiped his fingers on his jeans.

"I know," Ricky said. And then it hit him, this immediately sobering thought. Coming out of the canyon, his phone dinging with missed notifications as it reconnected to the cellular network. Just as data was delivered to the device, data would also be uploaded from it.

"Oh my god," he said. "Oh my god. Ben, you're a genius." His mind was suddenly clear. "I need to get back to campus."

Ricky hopped the hip-level iron fence and began running, not feeling anything. The alcohol in his brain and the stinging in his ankle both faded as he could only think of one thing.

They found her phone.

CHAPTER FIFTEEN

BREATHLESS AND STILL feeling slightly dizzy and nauseous, though the bite of the puking had worn off as he ran the mile back to campus, Ricky rapped his knuckles on Jordan's dorm door. After a few moments of more knocking, she answered the door.

"What is it?" she answered in an oversized t-shirt that went to her mid-thighs, her slender legs long and toned. She made a face of disgust. "Oh my god, Ricky. Have you been drinking?" The question came out with a maternal condemnation.

"A little," he admitted.

"A little? You smell like you barfed in a brewery."

He shook off her judgement. "I figured it out," he said, his words forced as he sucked in oxygen. "I need you to come with me."

"Figured what out? What are you talking about?" she folded her arms in front of her chest and leaned into the doorway.

"How we can find out what happened to Rachel. Come on!" he insisted.

Jordan's eyes widened. "Let me get some shorts on, hang on a second." She shut the door in his face and when she did a waft of melted wax hit his nose, making him feel slightly nauseous again. Ricky swallowed the saliva in his mouth and pushed it down his gullet, forcing any more vomit back down.

After a few moments she opened the door again. "Where are we going?" she asked.

"For the moment, to the computer lab," he said.

"Is it open this late?" she asked as they walked the hallway toward the entrance to the building and out in the cool night air.

"I have a keycard," he said.

"Where did you go tonight?" she asked him as he shuffled his feet in the dew-wet grass. They walked across the campus under the soft glow of the sidewalk lamps that lined the concrete walkways all across the university.

"Boot Scootin', with some guys from my Statistics class," he said.

She stopped in her tracks. "Wait. *You* went to the

Boot? With other people?"

He stopped as well. The incredulity in her voice was not lost on him. "Yeah. So what? I wanted to have a good time."

"Uh huh. You came back here from the canyon and decided to just go out to the country bar with a bunch of hicks?" Jordan asked.

"Oh, come on," he argued. It's not that—" as Ricky spoke, he felt it come up from his belly again and he doubled over, vomiting in the grass next to the sidewalk.

"Good lord, Ricky," she said. "How many beers did you have?"

"I don't know," he said. "I lost count." His knees shook under the weight of his palms resting on them.

"Are you sure you're good? Maybe we should just go back to the dorm and let you sleep this off. You're obviously drunk," she said.

"No," Ricky stood upright. "I mean, yes. I am probably a little tipsy. But I'm very certain we need to go to the computer lab."

"Whatever your plan is here, I hope we *do* find Rachel just so she can see this," Jordan shook her head in judgmental disgust.

"Yeah, well, I hope this actually works," Ricky said as he stumbled forward and to the doors of the computer lab. The lab jutted out from the main library, an afterthought of red brick attached to the graceful granite of the large and imposing library building. Pulling his keycard out of his wallet, Ricky held the thing to the door and it clicked, the light on the door lock mechanism flashing green.

Just inside, they descended a half-dozen steps and into the too-bright computer lab. Machines lined the walls, humming with a constant buzz. Fans, both box and oscillating, were strewn about as well, helping circulate the stuffy, warm air inside.

"Why is it so hot in here?" Jordan asked.

"The servers down here run really warm," Ricky said. "They're constantly having to be cooled."

"What do they do?"

Ricky pointed at one of the larger machines, a tower of black metal and blinking lights with countless cables running into and out of it. "That one is a firewall that I've been working on."

On one of the benches was a machine still out of a casing. Green circuit boards wired together, spidering off to other components littered the bench. Jordan picked it up in her hands. "I don't understand all this stuff," she said.

However, Ricky was already sitting in front of a computer monitor, the flat LED screen mounted to the wall above the bench. If she'd asked a question, he didn't hear her. He was plugged in. Opening the web browser on the machine, he pulled up a window and typed in an address.

Ricky had never considered himself religious. His brain was too scientific, too technological to accept the idea of an omnipotent creator somewhere out there pulling the strings on this planet.

But for the first time since he was a little boy, he prayed. He prayed that this would work. He prayed that he wasn't crazy.

Jordan inched up next to him at the workbench. "What are you doing?" she asked as he typed in the two-factor authentication code that had been sent to his phone.

"Okay, so you know how when we're down in the canyon, we can't get any cell phone signal?" Ricky asked.

"Yeah," she said.

"And when we come out, our phones start dinging like crazy with notifications?"

Her eyes widened as she began to understand what he was getting at. "Are you saying…" she trailed off.

"Exactly," he said matter-of-factly. "Rachel's phone backs up to the cloud. As soon as those guys down there turn it on outside of the canyon, it's going to start uploading all the new data."

Ricky logged in to the cloud storage web-based interface and clicked on an icon labelled photos. "I'm hoping she took pictures, something so we can see where she was before she disappeared."

"How do you know how to do all this?" Jordan asked, staring at the screen.

"You may find this hard to believe, but I didn't have a very social childhood," he replied sarcastically. "I've been building computers since I was in middle school."

On the screen, several pixelated images came into focus and Ricky clicked on one. It loaded and he looked at the metadata of the image. He didn't even need to cross-reference the date the image was taken to know.

"Bingo," he said. "They're uploading now."

The image downloaded and they both just stared at it.

"That's it, isn't it?" Ricky asked, not taking his eyes off the screen. "That's the cave?"

Dozens of primitive drawings, all red and black carved onto the grey rock of the cave, stared back at them. Ricky had seen these kinds of drawings in textbooks in school, but never like this. They looked undisturbed, almost new.

"She actually found it. Oh my god, this is amazing," Jordan moved closer to the screen. "Look at these," she pointed, "they're so detailed. Are there any more?"

Ricky clicked out of the cave drawings and back to the list of thumbnail images. Two more popped up as they were uploaded to the cloud. "They're still uploading," he said. "Quick, hand me that USB drive over there," he pointed to a thumb drive. Jordan handed it to him and, plugging it into the machine, mounted the drive and started transferring the images to it.

"Look at that one," Jordan said, pointing to a thumbnail.

Clicking on it, the image opened up, the face of a bison staring back at them. "This can't be right," Jordan said. "There haven't been bison in Palo Duro in nearly two hundred years."

In the background of the image, Ricky noticed something sticking up out of the brush and grass off in the distance. He zoomed in on it. "I don't remember seeing tents out there," he said. The tops of the tents were pointed, and even though grainy in the low light of the photo, he could tell that there were several. They would have seen them on the trail, especially with the fires that were prevalent around them in the picture.

Jordan shook her head. "Those aren't tents," she said. "Those are teepees."

"Teepees? Like, Native American teepees?" Ricky was perplexed. "I don't remember seeing teepees either."

"This is really weird," she said as she pulled out her cell phone.

"What are you doing?" Ricky asked.

"I'm calling Dr. Errington," she said, holding the device to her ear. After a few seconds, she perked up. "Hi, Dr. Errington. It's Jordan Harris. I know it's late, I'm so sorry. We—Rachel's brother and I—have something you need to see. Can we come to you? Okay. See you in thirty minutes."

She hung up the phone and Ricky pointed at the screen. "Look," he said as the pictures in the cloud backup folder began disappearing one by one. "They're deleting them."

"What? What do you mean deleting them?" Jordan leaned in, peering at the screen with him as the images disappeared from the folder one by one. "Why would they delete them?"

"Because there's something here they don't want us to see," Ricky said.

"That doesn't make sense."

"None of it does. But hopefully Dr. Errington can help."

"You got them?" she asked. "Before they got deleted?"

He pulled the USB drive from its socket on the front of the computer tower. "Right here."

"Do they know that we downloaded them? Like, can they track our IP address or something?"

"No. I'm behind a firewall and a VPN. Even if they knew someone had accessed the cloud system, it would take them a while to track where it came from," he said.

"Good," she said. "Now let's go. We're going to see Dr. Errington. Figure out exactly what is going on."

That missing limb pain Ricky had felt for the last four months reared its ugly head again and he hoped that he'd soon get some answers.

CHAPTER SIXTEEN

THE ANTHROPOLOGY PROFESSOR's home, a quaint cottage-style made of yellow brick with an archway on the front porch, was lit only by an incandescent bulb above the front door. The entire neighborhood, one of the older sections of town south of downtown and no more than a ten-minute drive from the university campus, was quiet except for the sound of Jordan's Rav4 as the brakes squealed when they pulled up to the front porch.

The smartwatch on Ricky's wrist lit up as he raised it to see the time. It was nearing close to one in the morning. The alcohol-induced vomiting and dizziness had subsided, and on their way to Dr. Errington's home, Jordan had stopped at a convenience store—

one of the few places in town open at this time—and bought him a fried burrito and a Gatorade. He ate the burrito and gulped down half of the salty electrolyte drink before they reached the professor's house.

"I'm never drinking again," he said, the back of his skull leaning as far into the headrest as it could go when they pulled up.

"You'll say that next time, too," she retorted with a half-smile. "But that's college."

As they got out of the vehicle and walked up the sidewalk that bisected the front lawn of the home, the grass perfectly manicured and green with new life, the front door opened, spilling a soft light from inside out onto the sidewalk.

The woman, who Ricky had not seen since the night Rachel went missing, was in a pair of pajama pants and a sweater with the university logo emblazoned across that swallowed her diminutive figure. Her greying dark hair was pulled back into a tight ponytail.

"Ms. Harris," Dr. Amelia Errington said, opening the doorway completely and ushering the two students inside, "I do hope this is important." Turning to Ricky, she gave him a once-over and he felt that she could sense the alcohol and tipsiness on him. She gave him a smile though. "Come in, come in," she said as they entered her living room.

Lit by a corner lamp above a slate metal desk, the

room was decorated in Native American relics. An ornamental headdress, colorful feathers and beads hanging from it, was mounted on one wall. A row of books was lined on a short shelf, bookended by small bison skulls. Ricky realized that there was no television in here, and aside from a MacBook on her desk, its clamshell screen closed, there was no technology in here at all.

"Thank you for meeting us this late, Dr. Errington," Jordan said. "I'm so sorry to bother you, but we have something you need to see."

The professor led them to her couch, an L-shaped sectional that hugged a coffee table the same color and build of her desk. Jordan explained how the park rangers down in the canyon had the area where Rachel had gone missing roped off.

"They found her cell phone," she said, finishing the story.

Dr. Errington simply shook her head, "And they still have no idea what happened to her?"

"Well, if they do, they won't tell us. But then, Ricky had an epiphany," she looked at Ricky.

He sat up. "Coming out of the canyon, I realized that our cell phones would reattach to the network and begin downloading information. Which means that they'd also start *uploading* information. Our phones automatically back up to the cloud."

The professor nodded. "But if they found her phone after all this time, how is it still working? Wouldn't it have gotten wet or something?"

"That's the thing," Jordan said. "Colton said it looked like it had just been dropped. Like, within the last day or so. And her initials were carved into the back metal."

"Carved?" Dr. Errington asked.

"Yeah, like with a stone," Jordan explained.

Ricky continued, "But with that information, I knew that if the sheriffs or the park rangers or investigators—or anyone—turned on that phone outside of the canyon, it would begin uploading data to the cloud. Including pictures that she would have taken. I thought if we could see any information on it, we could find out what happened to her."

"And we saw something confusing," Jordan said. "She took pictures, before she disappeared."

"Pictures of what?" Errington asked, her curiosity piqued.

"Well, that's why we're here. We need you to tell us what this is," Ricky held the USB drive out to her and the professor gingerly took it from his hand as if she were handling some long-lost artifact. "I copied the pictures from the cloud before they were erased."

"Erased?" The professor cocked her head with an eyebrow raised.

"Right. Whoever had the phone—sheriffs, park rangers—saw the pictures and began erasing them from the cloud backup," Ricky said.

"Why would they delete them? That doesn't make sense."

"Right. I think it's because she saw something that she wasn't supposed to see," Ricky answered.

Jordan nodded in agreement. "You need to look at those pictures, professor."

Errington reached over the back of her couch to the desk that hugged up against it and grabbed her silver slab of a laptop and slid a pair of glasses from the table on her face. She opened the screen and plugged the drive into one of its vacant USB ports. A window popped up on the display and she clicked on it, opening the folder for the drive.

There were four photo files and when Dr. Errington clicked on the first one, the image opening full-screen, she gasped. A rock wall, arched overhead of the shot, emblazoned with dozens of carvings and paintings displayed in the window.

"I can't believe it. I *don't* believe it," she muttered. "I came to teach here specifically to find this. This cave was a holy site to the Kiowa. Look at these carvings." She pointed to the screen. "This entire piece depicts the life and death of a day."

She described the various pictographs to them, and

Ricky felt a sense of amazement himself. These carvings, a bird swooping across the sky, a circle with rays that depicted the sun, various beasts and humans underneath, were not just a myth. Rachel had found this. She'd done what countless others had tried for years to no avail.

"And most cave paintings are done in black or red, but oxidized over the years. And whatever are found are usually contaminated with additional graffiti, usually kids who others who don't understand the historical importance of what they're messing with. But this looks like it hasn't been touched or seen in centuries." Leaning into the screen, Dr. Errington squinted her eyes. "And these are done in charcoal, yes, but look at the details. It's gold. These aren't just regular cave drawings. They have a religious aspect to them." She pointed out the glinting sparkles in the paintings.

She closed the file and opened the next.

The next picture opened and there, clear as day, was a bison, its dark fur surrounding tiny dark eyes beneath a pair of miniscule horns, staring right back at the camera.

"This can't be real," she said. "There haven't been bison in Palo Duro since the early eighteen hundreds. And there's no way she could have been so close to a wild one."

"Zoom in on the background," Jordan said. "It's

hard to see, but it's there."

The professor zoomed in on the background of the photo and shook her head. "No, no, no. This is a hoax. This can't be." She shut the lid of her laptop and stood up, placing the device on the coffee table in front of her. "This is ridiculous. It's," she looked at the clock, "nearly two o'clock in the morning and either I'm hallucinating or you two are trying to play a trick on me. Either way, I'm exhausted and it's time for you to go."

Jordan stood up. "We're serious! This is why we came to you because you would know what this is. Those were teepees in the background, weren't they?"

Errington shook her head. "This is ridiculous. I've been searching for that cave for half my life, and now you two are in my home with pictures that can't possibly be real. There haven't been teepees in that canyon in over two hundred years."

"But can't you see the confusion?" Jordan pleaded. "There *were* no teepees out there the night Rachel vanished. There were no bison. And that cave? Did the park rangers let you go to it? Because when we got close on the trail, they made us turn back." She looked at Ricky, who nodded. Jordan continued, "There's something weird about all this and we need your help."

"Dr. Errington," Ricky stood now, his voice quiet and meek. "I have this really weird feeling. And I don't think the question is, where did my sister go?" He paused, chewing on the inside of his cheek, trying to form the question. It sounded just as crazy out loud as it did in his head.

"It's *when* did she go?"

CHAPTER SEVENTEEN

BOTH THE PROFESSOR and Jordan looked at him, dumbfounded.

"Let's bring it back to reality, Ricky," Jordan said. "Rachel didn't fall in some time warp."

"It's Occam's Razor," Ricky said. "The simplest solution is quite often the right one. So are we to believe that she took these pictures—the bison, the teepee campground—and those things were moved out of the area before we got there? Without any prints or artifacts left behind?"

Both women looked at each other as Ricky worked through his thought process. He paced the floor in front of the coffee table.

He continued, "Or, did she find something in that

cave? Something that took her back to another time. A portal."

"But then how did her phone end up back here? That doesn't make any sense," Jordan said.

"Let me look at that cave painting again," Dr. Errington said. She sat back in front of the computer and opened its lid, the screen lighting up her face in the dim glow of the corner floor lamp.

She opened up the photo file of the cave paintings, their gold-streaked black figures etched into the brown rock and earth. Before her, the image opened up as she studied the markings. The birth and death of a day. The birds flying in the air above. The stick-figure humans dancing around a fire. The orb with rays surrounding it tracing across the sky in an oblong trace above the dancing humans, the canine figures and birds.

But there was more. More that she did not see at first glance.

Figures, golden streaks in the dark rock, dancing. A circle. And then human forms with the heads of birds and wolves.

"The old gods," the professor muttered.

"What?" Jordan asked. It was a phrase that Dr. Errington had used many times in the past.

"This isn't the birth and death of a day," the professor said, stunned. She fell back in the dining room chair and rubbed her temples. "This is instructions on how to communicate with the old gods. We've been wrong all along!" she exclaimed.

And then, to both Ricky and Jordan's surprise, Amelia Errington cocked her head back and laughed, this giddy noise coupled with tears streaming down her cheeks. Ricky knew they weren't tears of sorrow, though. These were the tears of a woman who'd spent her entire life searching for something and finally seeing it. Seeing that it wasn't just a myth, and it was much more than she'd ever dreamed.

Errington continued, wiping the tears from her cheeks, "This isn't just a cave. It *is* a portal. And, if your Occam's Razor theory is correct, it's a portal to another time."

Jordan now rolled her eyes and she paced the floor, "Do you two even hear yourselves? What you're talking about is impossible. Time travel?"

"Just as impossible as someone disappearing without a trace? Without so much as a hint of where they went?" Ricky asked. "As impossible as their phone showing up four months later, completely intact and working?"

Jordan looked at the floor, biting the inside of her cheek.

"I know, it sounds crazy," he continued, "but get rid of every other option. Get rid of every obstacle and the simplest answer is the right one."

Jordan shifted her gaze from him to Dr. Errington. "So what do we do?" she asked. "We can't waltz down to the canyon and just jump through a time warp."

"You're right," Errington said, "but I think you know someone who can get us down there without getting caught by the other authorities."

"You want to sneak down to an active crime investigation?" Jordan was indignant.

"Yeah, last time we tried that, I got cactus thorns all in my ankle," Ricky said. The last thing he wanted was Colton Graves pulling thorns out of his ankle with a pair of pliers again.

"Call him," the professor said coolly.

"If you say so," Jordan said. She pulled out her phone and dialed Colton's number. Holding the device to her ear as Ricky and the professor looked on hopefully, she said, "Hey babe. I know it's late and you've been working all night, but I really need you to come over to Dr. Errington's house." She paused for a few seconds. "No, no one is hurt, but I need you. We need you. Okay, see you soon."

Ricky sat on the couch, staring at the image on the screen, the cave paintings staring back at him. *We're coming, Rach*, he thought.

CHAPTER EIGHTEEN

COLTON WAS BEYOND exhausted and the last thing he wanted was to be awake. It had been nearly twenty-four hours since he last felt the warmth and comfort of the flannel sheets on his bed. And a long twenty-four hours it had been, out in the canyon, combing through brush and tagging anything that even looked like it could be mistaken as a footprint. The sun beat down on him all day and all he wanted was to go back home, take his boots off and crawl under those sheets.

He'd almost been there, too, when she called. A part of him wanted to just let it go to voicemail, but knowing Jordan, she'd then come knocking on his door, and like a band-aid ripping off a scabbed wound, better to just get it over with. Hearing her voice on the phone, he immediately regretted the decision.

She'd convinced him, however, with the words "we need you." She was at Dr. Errington's house, so maybe something terrible had happened. So he'd pulled his boots back on and drove into town—his house was a tiny, one bedroom trailer nearly halfway between the city and the canyon—to the anthropology professor's house.

Colton Graves had heard many tall tales in his short time as an employee of the Texas Parks and Wildlife Service. Hell, he'd heard more Sasquatch stories than he could recount, usually by campers nursing a bottle of bourbon wrapped in a brown bag or sitting next to a mountain of empty silver bullets. But now, he stared in almost annoyed disbelief at the computer screen in Dr. Errington's living room. He didn't even quite understand how the technology worked; how the pictures from the missing girl's phone were somehow on the internet and then transferred to Dr. Errington's computer. Multiple lapses in policy and procedure, most likely. The kind that would get a guy canned.

"Guys, this is ridiculous," he said. "There's no way these pictures were taken in Palo Duro. For one, the flora is all wrong. See how the mesquite brush here is all overgrown?" he pointed at an area of the screen. "We keep that to a minimum because their roots will choke out all the flowers. And two, there are no bison in the canyon. Not even accidentally. The nearest bison herd is nearly a hundred miles away."

"I didn't want to believe it myself," Dr. Errington said, sitting on her coffee table. "In fact, I don't know what to believe."

"So why am I here?" Colton asked.

Jordan sat next to him. "We need you to take us to the cave without being seen by anyone else," she said. "We need to find that cave, find these paintings," she clicked the screen, taking it back to the image Rachel took of the cave paintings.

"I can't do that," he said. "For one, it's an active crime scene. It's completely cut off, the whole trail, from the trailhead to the caves. There's no way we can get there without being seen. But let's say we're able to sneak past whoever has been left on duty, the moment we disturb the crime scene, we are immediately suspects in her disappearance. I lose my job, you two," he looked at Jordan and Ricky, "will lose your scholarships—probably be expelled—and you," to Dr. Errington, "can say goodbye to your tenure."

"Fine," Ricky said with an air of false defiance so thin that anyone could see right through it, "we'll go without you."

"Please," Colton snorted. "Make sure to take your own pliers this time."

Jordan grabbed Colton's hands and held them between her own, interlacing their fingers. "I know, it
sounds crazy, but we need your help. Clearly you can
see something isn't right here. These pictures," she
pointed to the computer, "came from her phone. They
show something that shouldn't exist, because it *doesn't*
exist—anymore."

"Because she took them in the past," Ricky said.

Colton threw his hands up, releasing from Jordan's
soft grip. "You can't actually believe that," he said, rolling his eyes. At this point, he was ready to leave and
not discuss this any further. He'd even not be so flabbergasted at Jordan and Ricky believing this non-
sense—people who have experienced trauma such as a
missing person will make up all kinds of scenarios in
which their loved ones are still alive. But the fact that
the professor was cosigning this outlandish theory
threw him for a loop.

Facing the front door for a moment, contemplating
leaving, Colton ran his hands through his hair. A yawn
escaped his mouth. He turned to face the three of
them, looking as if he were a new recruit in a bank rob-
bery. "Guys, I know you want to find her. We do, too.
But this is just too much. It's not *Back to the Future* out
there," he said.

And with that, Colton kissed Jordan on the cheek
though she pulled away from him.

"I can't believe you're not going to help us with this," she whispered. The tears welling in her eyes began to drip down her cheeks.

"I'm sorry," he said.

He said goodnight to Dr. Errington and to Ricky, neither of whom said much of a response and he walked back out to his vehicle. Turning the ignition of his pickup, the engine sputtered before settling into a hum. Colton yanked the shifter into drive, knowing that things were now in motion that he couldn't stop.

But, he had an obligation to try.

CHAPTER NINETEEN

RICKY WOKE UP to the sound of a crow cawing outside the window and, opening his eyes, took him a moment to remember where he was. Clutching a patchwork quilt, he stretched his legs out, the joints in his knees and hips stiff from sleeping in a curled-up position on Dr. Errington's couch.

The world came alive as he blinked himself awake. The blue jays on the branches of the pecan trees chirping outside. The smell of percolating coffee. The sounds of women's voices coming from the kitchen. He sat up on the couch and could feel his hair sticking in every direction.

One of the two women in the kitchen, sitting at the breakfast table in the nook tucked away in the corner must have noticed his shuffling, because he heard, "Hey sleepyhead, get over here."

As he stood up from the couch, Ricky immediately noticed his head and a splitting headache pounding in his temples.

"God, I feel terrible," he said.

"That's called a hangover," Jordan chuckled. "Sit down." She pulled one of the two vacant chairs out from under the round dining table and he did as he was told. "I'll get you some coffee."

The sunlight filtering through the open blinds was bright and it hurt to look at it. In the light and on the table's chipping surface was an unfolded map. Even from his viewing angle, he could see that it was a map of the canyon and surrounding areas.

After a few seconds, Jordan returned to the table with a white porcelain mug that had the maroon university emblem stamped on the side. He took a sip, the steam floating up his face from the cup and felt the warmth flow down his throat.

"What are you two looking at here?" he asked.

Dr. Errington sat back in her seat. "The canyon, and how to bypass the park rangers to get down to the caves." She sounded so sure of herself. At one time, not that long ago, he'd have protested, told them *no way*. Now, however, he was all ears.

"What are you suggesting?" he asked, taking another sip from his mug.

"Well, as you know, the state park itself ends just beyond the boulder garden trail," Dr. Errington said. "With the caves on private land, we don't even have to go through the park." She pushed the map toward him and followed a path with her finger. "This is a private road, but we should be able to get to it from the main highway. After that, it's just a two, maybe three mile hike to the cave system."

"We go tonight," Jordan said, hovering over the map as well.

"Why tonight?" Ricky asked. "After Colton left last night, he could have told the sheriffs or Chet Smallbone. We'll be caught."

Dr. Errington spoke up, "It has to be tonight. Look at the pictograph." She turned her computer to him, the image of the cave drawings on the screen. "See the figures in a circle? They're performing a ritual to open the portal to communicate with their old gods. Under a full moon."

Ricky began to understand. "And tonight's the full moon," he stated. Dr. Errington nodded.

Ricky pursed his lips. The prospect of hiking three miles in the dark made him clench up, though he knew what to look out for now, and would have a little more prep time instead of being pulled out of the car like he'd been the day before. "Here's my biggest concern," he said. "You said you've been looking for this cave for twenty years. How do you know we'll be able to even find the portal, or whatever Rachel found? She may have come across it mistakenly."

"Well, frankly, I don't," Dr. Errington said. "But, we have some pretty good clues in front of us. We know where she went, for one. We know where the caves themselves are. We'll have the three of us to look for rock formations or anything that looks familiar from her photos."

Ricky, perhaps from the caffeine that helped his thumping headache, which now subsided to more of a dull ache, had a moment of clarity. "Can I see your computer again?"

Dr. Errington crossed the room and brought back the laptop, which Ricky opened and pulled up the photographs from the USB drive. Jordan, her interest piqued at what Ricky was doing, scooted her chair along the hardwood floor up next to him. He brought up one of the photos, the one of the cave drawings and opened a command line window.

"What are you doing?" she asked.

"I don't know why I didn't think of this before," he said. "But I can actually see, in the metadata, the exact coordinates where these pictures were taken," he explained as he typed in a command in the terminal.

Ricky hit the return key and a list of information scrolled on the screen. "This is how companies like Google and Facebook know where your picture was taken. It's all here in the data."

Scrolling through the data for a second, he said, "Here it is," and Dr. Errington came to his side as he was sandwiched between the two women staring at the screen. The professor grabbed a pen and began scribbling the coordinates in a corner of the map.

"How did you learn all this stuff?" she asked.

Ricky just shrugged. "I didn't have very many friends growing up. Rachel was always doing something to get her hands dirty while I was taking stuff apart, learning how it worked."

"Well, it's a gift," Dr. Errington said with an affirming smile.

"So what now?" Ricky asked. "We just wait til tonight?"

"Sort of," Dr. Errington said. "We need to get supplies together. And get some rest. It may be another long night."

Jordan nodded. "We'll need to get you some proper hiking shoes," she said to Ricky, "but I'm sure you could probably use a little more sleep."

She was right. He felt like he'd been hit by a bus. His joints ached and an uncommon exhaustion coupled with the nausea of the minor hangover had him feeling groggy and sluggish. He wanted to go back to his dorm, shut the windows and curl under the sheets on his full-size bed that was much more comfortable than the anthropology professor's leather couch.

"That sounds good to me," he agreed.

"Perfect," Jordan said. "I'll grab some packs, you get some rest, and we'll meet back up here around nine tonight. Sound good?"

Ricky and Dr. Errington both agreed.

On the drive back to campus, Ricky hoped he could rest. His mind was going ninety miles an hour, still holding a hint of disbelief that they'd discovered what happened to Rachel. He needed sleep, but something told him it would come at a struggle.

CHAPTER TWENTY

THOUGH THE SUNSETS, bathing the expansive panhandle sky in glorious hues of pinks and gold, came later and later in the evening as spring continued its march out of the gloom of winter, the sun had long disappeared beneath the western horizon, leaving behind a glinting starfield. Completely cloudless and with a moon shining bright and high in the sky, the night air was cool as Ricky and Jordan threw their backpacks in the back of Dr. Errington's white Jeep Cherokee.

They had reconvened here at the professor's house just after nine. From the house, the lights that hovered above the baseball field on campus could be seen glowing in the distance and Ricky thought he could even hear a faint cheer or two, the sound like static that swelled and then quickly dissolved.

"Ricky, let's go," Jordan said, and he turned back to the vehicle and climbed in the back seat. The upholstery, canvas and cloth, was worn in areas and dried mud caked the floorboard.

"Sorry it's a bit messy back there," Dr. Errington said as she pulled the lever beside her into reverse and backed out of the driveway. "Been a bit muddy on the bike trails this season."

Ricky wiped some dirt from his pants and told her he didn't mind. All three of them were dressed completely in black and it made him feel like a trio of thieves, going out to rob a convenience store. Behind him in the Jeep's cargo area, their three backpacks were stuffed with supplies—water, flashlights and a hatchet, as well as a first aid kit. The plan was simple: find the caves and, using the coordinates from the metadata embedded in Rachel's photos, find the portal.

And then, extraction.

It dawned on Ricky, now that he had a moment to think about what they were actually planning on doing. It sounded crazy. Time portals. Logically, such a thing shouldn't exist. But, it was Einstein that had proven the theory of wormholes. It was Arthur C. Clarke that had written that any sufficiently advanced technology is indistinguishable from magic. Perhaps, then, that's what this was—some form of technology or scientific anomaly that no one could explain—at least not with their current understanding of the universe.

According to Dr. Errington, the portal was a myth of ancient Native American culture, a way for them to communicate with their gods. As they drove out of town, past the campus and the baseball field, the stands and bleachers full of maroon and white, Ricky wondered what gods they would find waiting for them in the portal.

The drive from the city to the canyon was about twenty miles and for the most part, was void of any chit-chat among the three of them in the vehicle. Flashing lights from behind them illuminated the car and Dr. Errington cursed under her breath.

"I wasn't speeding or anything," she said, slowing down and pulling the Jeep onto the shoulder, her tires crunching on the loose gravel.

The vehicle behind them pulled up and the officer got out and walked up to the passenger's door. Without even rolling down the window, they could see that it wasn't a sheriff, but a park ranger—Colton Graves.

Jordan rolled down the window guiltily and didn't say anything.

"I figured I'd see y'all heading out this way. Went to the professor's house and your car was there but hers wasn't," he said.

"We've got to at least try," Jordan said. "We've got

to find where she went."

"I know," Colton said. "Which is why I'm here. I can get you to the caves without being seen by Sheriff Jones's men or Smallbone."

The three of them in the Jeep let out a collective sigh. "But if we're caught, you'll get in trouble," Jordan protested. "We can make it."

"I'm sure you could. But let me help. I want to find her just as much as you do," he said.

They agreed.

"Follow me," Colton said. "We're going to take a couple of backroads that hug the north side of the canyon. There's an old service trail on the ranch side that can take us to the floor. Then we can hike down." Getting back in his truck, he pulled around them in the road and waited for the professor to pull her Jeep onto the two-lane blacktop. He led them for about three miles until his brake lights lit up in bright red and he turned onto an unmarked dirt road that jutted off the highway proper.

Dust and dirt kicked up from their tires on the dry unpaved service road and they slowed down as the road curved and wound through shapeless farm land. After a few more minutes, Colton pulled his pickup off the trail and exited, waiting outside the open door for them to do the same.

Dr. Errington turned off her vehicle and Ricky began handing them the backpacks from the cargo hold. Ricky, grabbing his own backpack, which was an older North Face pack that the professor had in her garage, slung the thing over his shoulders and surveyed the flatness ahead of him.

"It's crazy to believe that there's a canyon out there," he said.

"Imagine what the Spaniards must have thought when they marched through this area," Dr. Errington said. "All this nothingness, and then..." she trailed off.

"Where are we?" Jordan asked.

"We're on the north side of the canyon. It's going to be about a three-mile hike down the service trail and then we'll be able to access the caves from the far side. The county guys are mounted up around here, but we'll be able to move around them," Colton said.

They marched single-file down the service trail that intersected the dirt road, Ricky careful to keep his eyes open for any outlying cactus plants that threatened his ankles. He swept his flashlight back and forth as he pulled up the rear of their party. In the distance, a coyote howled, joined by others, the high-pitched barks and yips breaking up the heavy silence.

Despite his experience with the cactus, he was beginning to understand what drew his sister and Jordan to the outdoors. It was absolutely beautiful out here, in a way he couldn't quite comprehend yet still felt in his core.

After hiking for nearly thirty minutes, he could see, on the horizon and getting closer, the canyon opening up ahead of them. Soon, the four of them reached the edge of the ridge. At some points, it was a straight drop, nearly a thousand feet, to the canyon floor.

"Alright, the service trail to the floor is a little further this way," Colton said, pointing them to a section of the trail just a few hundred yards away.

Ricky froze. He was okay with hiking on one of the trails like this. But, looking down at the vastness of the canyon and the cliffs that dropped off into the void made his hands clench and his heart start beating hard, the muscles in his chest tightening.

Almost as if she could sense his hesitation, Jordan turned back to him. "It's okay," she said. "We're with you."

"It's just, one small misstep and you're dead," he said, gulping.

"So don't misstep," she said with a wink.

"Got to keep it quiet back there," Colton called out in a half-whisper. "Come on." He continued to lead them toward the edge of the canyon where, close to one of the sheer drop-off cliffs that made Ricky clench up, a switchback trail was cut into the sloping edge of the canyon wall. They went down the trail single-file, loose dirt and rocks occasionally slipping under Ricky's feet. He didn't like the feeling of being off balance, but he kept himself upright on the trail, slowly making his way down as the caboose of this train.

After another twenty minutes, they were on level ground. Ricky sighed his relief.

"We're on the north side of the caves now," Colton said. "This is all private land, so there aren't any clear-cut trails. Stay behind me and keep your lights on low. We don't want to attract attention out here." He continued tramping through the brush, using a machete to swipe away any errant mesquite brush that inhibited their path to the caves.

Ricky kept his flashlight still at his feet, relying on the light and sounds of the others as his guide. He really didn't want another run-in with a cactus out here. "Dr. Errington," he whispered. The woman cocked an ear his way. "How did the Spanish make it through all this wilderness?"

"Much like we are now," she said quietly. "There were trading routes set up between tribes, not unlike the dirt trails we've made today. But this land is inhospitable in places." Even in the darkness, he could tell the woman was beaming, getting to discuss the early pre-Columbian life of the native tribes that inhabited this land. She slowed and sidled next to him and continued, "Coronado and his men basically circled themselves in the panhandle for nearly two weeks. They were even caught up in a tornado southeast of here."

"I remember reading that," Jordan said over her shoulder. "I've been wanting to go down to Caprock Canyon and do some digging for artifacts."

"What's Caprock Canyon?" Ricky asked.

"It's another canyon system about two hundred miles southeast of here," Jordan said. "The Spanish met up with some tribes down there as well."

"The movement of the Spanish during the age of the conquistador is prevalent all through this area," Dr. Errington said. "Many people think that the United States was settled in New England and then Europeans eventually migrated westward. However, the Spanish were here for nearly two centuries before the United States gained its independence. In those two centuries, trade routes were established. Entire cities were built."

"What happened to it all?" Ricky asked.

"The Spanish lost the war against America and the victor is the one that writes the history books. Take my classes sometime," she said. "I think you'll find it all very interesting."

As they spoke and conversed in hushed tones, Ricky never realized how much ground they'd covered until Colton raised his right hand, elbow cocked at ninety degrees to signal them to stop.

"We're going to have to cross the river up ahead. There's a wooden bridge set up, but it's very unstable and we'll have to cross one at a time. I will go first, and then Dr. Errington. Ricky, you come next and then Jordan. Got it?" he asked.

The three of them nodded their heads in agreement.

Ricky could hear the water gurgling in the stream a few hundred yards ahead and they approached the bridge in just a few minutes' hike. Ricky looked at the bridge and gulped. Unstable was an understatement. The ropes that threaded the planks looked frayed from years of exposure. There looked to be several planks missing. One misstep and you would be in the water, carried down river.

However, Colton went first, holding on to the ropes on his left and right and walking carefully on the planks until he'd reached the other bank. Dr. Errington followed suit, slower than the park ranger, but also made it.

"Okay, Ricky," Colton called out.

Behind him, Jordan tapped him on the small of the back with her palm. "It's alright. Just do as they did. Both hands on the ropes," she told him.

He approached the rope bridge, the thing swaying gently in the cool night breeze. Beneath his feet, the river flowed without stopping or regard for his fear.

Gripping the ropes at his sides, Ricky stepped onto the first plank and it swayed. He nearly fell over sideways, but he steadied himself and, pulling his other foot from dry and secure ground, took another step onto the bridge. One foot in front of the other, he walked slowly, keeping his hands on the ropes, though the strands hurt his palms and stuck to him like splinters in wood.

Nearly halfway through, he stepped on a plank and it snapped under his weight. Ricky felt his body shift and his leg slip through the new hole and he gripped the ropes instinctively, his hands stinging from the weathered strands.

"Ricky!" Jordan called out.

"I'm," he started, pulling himself up. "I'm okay." Steadying himself again, he continued walking across the bridge, finally making it to the other side, joining the professor and Colton.

"Okay, Jordan!" Colton called out, and they watched as Jordan gracefully, without a hitch, made it across the rope bridge, stepping over the broken plank that Ricky had nearly fallen through.

"Showoff," Ricky elbowed her and she gave him a proud smile.

"Alright, the caves are just over this ridge," Colton said. "Again, it's a steep climb down, so keep your feet steady. Slow steps down and make sure your footing is secure before going on." With Jordan and Dr. Errington both skilled hikers, Ricky knew that Colton was really speaking directly to him.

Jordan walked directly in front of Ricky and she tested her footing with each step as they walked over the ridge. He followed suit, feeling the rocks beneath his feet shift. The backpack on his shoulders felt heavy and the weight made his muscles ache, but he continued hiking over the ridge.

Ahead of them, no more than a few hundred yards, Ricky could see the caves, dark recesses in the landscape. Yellow crime scene tape, still roping off the area, fluttered in the air surrounding them. The last time he'd been out here was that cold autumn night, and the emotions welled up in him. More than anything, he wanted to run out, sprint to the caves and find the place where his sister disappeared. He kept his head about him though. At the mouth of the cave system, they'd check the coordinates from Rachel's pictures against their positioning and then find the place she'd gone.

Colton pulled up the yellow tape and the three of them ducked underneath. Now, all four of them congregated in the flat area in front of the caves. He then turned toward the open maw and called out.

"Okay," Colton said loudly, "they're all here."

Ricky looked to Jordan and Dr. Errington, confusion on their faces. From the darkness of the cave, a silver pistol glinted in the moonlight. Attached to the pistol was a hand. Chet Smallbone appeared from the darkness. He held the gun steady on the three of them.

"Colton," Jordan stammered, "what's going on here?"

He turned to her. "I'm sorry," he said. "We couldn't risk it."

"Risk what?" Jordan asked, though her question went unanswered.

Dr. Errington was much less confused and more indignant. "Chet, what the hell are you doing? Put that gun down."

He kept the gun on them despite her protests. "I'm sorry, Amelia. This is how it has to be. Outsiders aren't allowed in these caves. That's how it's been for a thousand years."

Ricky was still more confused than frightened, despite the weapon pointed at them, though he remained quiet. The last thing he wanted was to spook the park ranger. "Sir," he asked calmly. "My sister went in those caves and we think we can find a way to bring her back."

"I know. And I'm here to tell you that that's not going to happen," Chet Smallbone said.

CHAPTER TWENTY ONE

"WHAT'S GOING ON, Chet?" Amelia Errington asked, her hands held up at her shoulders, palms facing the park ranger holding a gun.

"I suggest you three turn around and go back home. There's nothing here for you," Smallbone said. His eyes were hidden beneath the brim of his green cap, keeping half his face in shadow.

Jordan was much less calm. "Colton, tell him to put the gun down. Please." The last word implied a desperation that was palpable among the two students and the professor.

"Why did you bring us all the way down here, just to tell us to leave?" Dr. Errington asked.

"We knew that you were getting close and we

needed to stop you before you made a mess of things," Smallbone said. "We wanted to show you that we are serious about this hallowed ground. No one steps foot in these caves."

"But my sister did," Ricky said.

"Exactly. And you see what happened to her," Smallbone retorted.

"But we have proof that she's still alive," Ricky said. "The pictures, from her phone. We've seen them. Rachel found something, a portal through time."

Jordan nodded, "All we want is to bring her back. We won't say anything to anyone after this. We just want to get Rachel back."

"That's not going to be possible. Every time the portal is disturbed, the energy that powers it gets diminished. Our job for generations has been to protect the energy of the old gods," Smallbone said. "We must protect this place, because once it diminishes in our time, it disappears in all time. Our ancestors, my people who lived here long before the Europeans came to this land, guarded the portal for those who would come after them, and now we do the same."

"Rachel went through though," Ricky said. "And the portal is still here."

"But she hasn't returned. Her accidental discovery could have destroyed the portal forever," Smallbone said.

"Her phone came back through though," Ricky continued, his hands held up to his sides. "The portal is still open. The energy still exists. Please, just let us attempt. Worst case scenario, we die in the past and you won't worry about us telling anyone about this cave."

Smallbone shook his head. "And risk the publicity if three more people go missing here? There's already enough disturbance here as it is. We have worked too hard to draw attention away from this place."

"What do you mean, *draw attention away*?" Ricky had a sudden thought. Everything began to click into place in his mind. "The jacket," he said. "The one the divers found. That wasn't hers, was it?"

"Smart boy," Smallbone said. "We couldn't have the search teams getting too close to this place. It's too sacred. Now turn around and go home. There's nothing here for you."

Dr. Errington turned to Ricky and Jordan. "He's right. There's nothing more we can do," she said haughtily.

Ricky nearly did a double-take. She couldn't possibly be giving up this easily. Despite the park ranger holding a gun to them, they had come so close and figured out what happened to Rachel. They couldn't just turn around now, after they'd come so far. "But, professor," he started to object, but she wove a hand his way, shushing him.

"May we ask that Mr. Graves escort us back to our vehicle?" Dr. Errington asked.

"No," Smallbone answered quickly. "I believe you will be able to adequately retrace your way back to where you came from."

"And I believe you're right, Chet." Still with her hands held high, she motioned to Ricky and Jordan, and, keeping their eyes on the park ranger holding the weapon, slowly made their way backward and away from the cave entrance.

As they trekked away, Ricky was fuming. All he wanted to do was rush the entrance, find the portal and bring his sister back from the past. They were so close. Why did Colton sell them out? Once they were far enough away from the caves and, continuously looking back, finally convinced they weren't being followed, he finally spoke.

"What the hell was all that about?" he asked.

Without turning to face him, Dr. Errington, who led the way back through the untamed brush and overgrowth of the canyon answered, "Something we should have expected."

Ricky was confused. "Then why didn't we?"

"Just keep walking and be quiet," Dr. Errington said. "I have a plan."

"What's the plan? Run away and don't die?" he

asked, trudging over a mesquite brush. The thorns ripped at his clothing and Ricky furiously thrashed until he was free of it.

Dr. Errington turned to him and he stopped in his tracks. He was breathing heavily and he was so angry he could feel his heartbeat behind his ears.

"I need you to calm down for a minute and understand that I've got this under control," the professor said.

"Yeah, well, unless you have something up your sleeve, all I see is that we've been caught and double-crossed and now Rachel is going to be stuck in the past forever." Ricky seemed to get louder with every syllable as he spoke until he was nearly screaming. He continued, flailing his arms and kicking at shrubs. "And why did Colton set us up like that? This is horseshit!"

"Ricky," Jordan said, "calm down and listen to Dr. Errington."

"No, *you* listen," he said. "It's *my* sister we're talking about here. For months I've wanted nothing than to find her. And we're this close. *This close.* And for what? To just turn around?"

Dr. Errington remained calm and quiet during this tirade. Once Ricky calmed down, she said, "Are you done? Because I want you to listen to me. This has to happen tonight. Smallbone fell for my bluff and left us out here alone, so we've still got a chance to make this happen. If my theories are correct, the portal opens only on a full moon. This is going to be very dangerous and there's a chance it won't work. But, first I need to know." She paused and pointed toward the river that ran beside them, the water rushing over rocks and boulders in the riverbed. "Can you swim?"

Ricky's eyes went wide as he looked at the river as well, remembering where it flowed.

Directly to the cave.

CHAPTER TWENTY TWO

"GIVE ME YOUR backpacks," Dr. Errington instructed them. Ricky and Jordan did as she asked, and though Ricky now felt naked and vulnerable without their supplies, he knew this would be the only way they'd be able to get to the caves.

At the bank of the river, they each hugged the professor, who was now loaded down with their backpacks.

"Be safe," Jordan said to Dr. Errington.

"You two as well. And listen to me," she said, looking at both of them. "Don't stop. Go all the way to the caves. I'll do my part. I'll see you both in another time."

With that, Dr. Errington turned and trudged back up through the canyon toward her vehicle on the ridge, and Ricky and Jordan started toward the river, all alone under the dark sky. Then, they began to undress, taking off their boots and clothes until they were down to their underwear. He tied the strings of his boots in a knot and hung them around his neck. Ricky kept his eyes averted from Jordan, and when he did look at her, consciously kept his eyes above her neckline. Jordan's eyes, however, were locked on him.

"What?" he asked, confused.

"I just would have never thought you had so much muscle under your clothes. Are you secretly working out?" she asked.

He blushed and didn't answer. Instead, he motioned to the water. "Are you ready?"

Holding their clothing high above their heads, they stepped into the water. As soon as they waded in, Ricky gasped. It was even colder than he'd anticipated and it took him by surprise. As they waded in deeper, the cold aching down to his bones, Ricky breathed in and out, keeping himself calm and steady as the water rushed past them. He kept his footing secure by ensuring each foot was planted before taking another step and, after a few minutes, he was confident in walking against the current.

Behind him, Jordan's teeth chattered, the water getting deeper the further they waded. They silently made their way upstream, Ricky leading the way. He turned occasionally to ensure Jordan was still behind him and she hurried her pace to walk next to him.

"I've never felt anything this cold in my life," she said quietly.

"Me neither," Ricky said, though he felt his body acclimating to the coldness, only occasionally getting a shock when the water would lap up above his stomach, touching otherwise dry parts of his body.

Out of the corner of his eye, he saw movement and stopped in his tracks, grabbing Jordan's arm. She peered over to the bank and they stood silently as a deer walked out of the brush and to the water's edge. They watched as the deer lapped water from the river. Behind it, two more deer, both smaller than the first, came up beside the first.

"Wow," Jordan whispered.

A coyote howled in the distance and the deer with its two companions left the river and walked back into the brush. Ricky and Jordan continued down the river.

"That was awesome," he said.

"There's all kinds of wildlife out here. It's really cool to see them in their habitat. We're the intruders here," she said. And then, "I hope we are getting close. I don't think I can handle much more of this."

As if on cue, they turned a bend in the stream, and the ridge where the cave resided stood off no more than a hundred yards in the distance. "There it is!"

Ricky exclaimed hoarsely.

He could see the police tape reflecting the little light from the moon above them, but it seemed otherwise abandoned. Dr. Errington's plan had worked, at least up to now. Colton and Chet had left, with the cave's entrance itself left unguarded. They climbed out of the river and, shivering, shook the water off their bodies, hoping to somewhat dry off before putting their clothes back on. Having his body covered again helped immensely, though. Ricky pulled the hood of his sweater above his head to keep his body temperature contained.

"I can't believe we made it," Jordan said. "I felt like a popsicle in there."

"I'm just glad to be out of the water. I kept thinking a fish was going to come and bite my toes." This made Jordan giggle and Ricky cocked his head. "Don't laugh at me. It's a real fear," he said jokingly.

They sat on the ground, huddled together near the bank of the river, to get their body temperatures back up. She leaned into him, his arms wrapped around her. Her teeth chattered and he rubbed his hands over her arms to generate heat. Once they were sufficiently dry, the two got up and started hiking toward the mouth of the caves.

"Check our coordinates," he said to Jordan, who pulled out her electronic GPS device. "We're north of where she took the picture of the cave drawings, so we should be able to go into the caves and go due south."

"Dr. Errington said she's been searching for this place for twenty years. How are we going to know when we find it?" Ricky asked.

"I don't know. We'll just follow the coordinates and hope we're going the right direction," she answered. Not as positive a response as he'd have liked, but they approached the caves anyway. The entrance was dark, and they didn't have much more than a pocket flashlight to light their way. The LED bulb in the light shone brightly on the walls as they curved above their heads. The entrance was wide, and at least eight feet high, but it got narrower and shorter the further back they went.

"How did Rachel even know where to go in here? It's so dark," Ricky said.

"I don't think she did," Jordan said. "She must have found it accidentally."

"She must have, because this just looks like an empty cave to me." As they spoke, their voices echoed in the chamber.

As they explored further back into the caves, they had to hunch over and eventually crawl on their hands and knees. Ricky hoped they'd find the chamber with the golden paintings soon because he was beginning to feel claustrophobic. What he thought was water dripping down his forehead was sweat, and he wiped his brow on his sleeve.

With his head turned to the side, he saw a glinting of light to his left. "Hey, can you check our coordinates again?" he asked to Jordan, crawling behind him.

Wriggling in the tight space of the cave, she pulled out her electronic GPS unit. The backlit dot matrix screen lit up and she said, "We're here. Or close. This is it."

"Follow me." Ricky turned toward the glinting of light through a sliver-like opening that he barely fit through. Inside the new cavern, he could stand. The room was lit by cracks in the earth above shining through, illuminated by the full moon.

Jordan came behind and gasped. There, in front of them, the wall of paintings and carvings displayed in their glory.

"I don't believe it," Jordan said, her voice trailing off. They examined the carvings, dark red and black hues complimented with gold outlines.

"So this is what she was after," Ricky said as he reached up, running his fingers on the wall. "It's beautiful." He took a step back from the wall to examine it as a whole. It was covered with primitive drawings of bison and deer, along with the river. The moon, an orb of gold and black above, was depicted with rays of gold and red shooting down to the pictographs. In the middle of it all, a group of stick figures, their arms interlinked around a fire, their heads pointed to the moon above. *Communicating with the old gods.*

Technology and magic.

Jordan tugged on his arm. To their right, a man-sized opening in the cave spilled to the outside world. "Do you think we've gone through? Do you think we're..." he looked out of the opening.

"There's only one way to find out," she said.

CHAPTER TWENTY THREE

CHET SMALLBONE DROVE along the single two-lane highway out of the canyon and Colton Graves sat in the passenger seat of the pickup truck. He had remained relatively quiet as they drove to the place where he'd left his truck. He thought it foolish to allow them to leave on foot alone, though Smallbone felt that they'd been scared and warned enough that the professor and the students wouldn't try to come back. To be sure, he posted one of the sheriff's deputies as well as a volunteer firefighter close to trail near the cave as a precaution.

Colton was also upset with the way his boss chose to handle the altercation. He thought the gun was excessive, but he did understand the importance of protecting the cave and the portal from outsiders. For nearly a century, the park rangers had been guardians of that holy ground. Before that, the duty was passed on through generations of the remnants of Native American families, with Chet Smallbone the last of his kind.

After Smallbone, the bloodline ended.

As he drove, heading back to the dirt road where he'd instructed Graves to leave his truck, Smallbone fiddled with the radio, eventually landing on some music. Colton assumed his displeasure with his boss was palpable.

As if his boss could read his thoughts, Smallbone finally spoke, "They were getting too close."

"They've got good intentions, Chet," Colton said. He never used his superior's first name in conversation.

"I know they do. Nobody, aside from her family of course, wants that girl to be found alive more than me. But we can't have people in the sacred land," he said.

"We could have done it differently," Colton argued.

"Well, nonetheless—" he was cut off by the blinding lights of a vehicle cresting a hill in front of them. "Damn, turn off your brights."

They noticed the vehicle driving erratically and at an

alarming speed. In a moment, the car zoomed past them.

"By god," Chet said, "I think that was—"

Colton whipped his head and turned in his seat to see the white Jeep Cherokee continuing along the highway. "It was, sir. It was them!"

Slamming on the brakes, Chet Smallbone's truck fishtailed and he turned the truck in the road, the tires crunching on the loose asphalt of the shoulder. He accelerated, pressing his foot nearly through the floorboard causing his truck to whine in protest before settling down.

Amelia Errington's taillights were several hundred yards in the distance now, and the park rangers raced to catch up with her.

"What the hell are they doing?" Smallbone asked, more to himself than to Colton.

But Colton knew what they were doing. They were hoping to catch the park rangers off-guard and make another run at the cave. "They know that we expect them on the back trails, not through the main gate," he said. "That's where they're heading."

The pickup's engine revved as Smallbone kept his foot heavy on the gas pedal. Coming over a hill, Colton felt his stomach lurch up through chest, the momentary weightless feeling when falling.

They'd almost caught up with the professor and her

students when, inexplicably, the Jeep made a u-turn on the highway. Smallbone threw his foot on the brake pedal, their tires squealing. He accelerated again toward the professor's vehicle. The Jeep came at them once more however, the headlights bright and blinding. A dangerous game of chicken, both the Jeep and the park ranger's truck were in the same lane.

"Chet, look out!" Colton exclaimed, instinctively reaching out to the dashboard and bracing himself from the inevitable collision. However, both vehicles swerved at the last moment and the Jeep fishtailed again, stopping in the shoulder. Colton could see, once the dust had settled and the Jeep came to a complete stop, that the front driver's side tire had blown, the rubber sagging depressingly against the aluminum wheel.

Smallbone yanked the shifter into park and got out of the truck, looking up and down the road for any incoming traffic. Colton released his white-knuckled grip on the dash and his seat belt and followed suit. They approached the Jeep cautiously and saw Dr. Errington in the driver's seat, laughing hysterically.

"What is so damn funny, Amelia?" Chet Smallbone demanded. "You're gonna get someone killed out here. Get out of the vehicle, all of you. You're under arrest."

In the driver's seat, Colton could see the professor, her wavy brunette curls wild in every direction. At her side in the passenger's seat, Jordan sat still, her hoodie pulled over her head, probably scared witless from what just occurred. In the back, Colton could make out Ricky's shape and hoodie through the dark tinted windows.

"Get out of the car," Smallbone said, opening the driver's door. "Hands where I can see them."

The woman, still laughing, though more controlled did as he asked.

"You two as well," the park ranger demanded, though both stayed in place, neither moving. "Come on," he reiterated. "Get out."

Turning his attention to the professor who leaned against the fender, sitting low due to the blown tire, Smallbone asked her, "What do you think you're doing? Thought you'd give it the ol' college try?"

"You are so dense, Chet," she answered. "Of course not."

"Then what are you doing?"

A tight-lipped grin struck across her face, the look a small child gets just before they do something they know will get them in trouble. "Stalling you."

Colton whipped his head, his eyes meeting his superior's as they simultaneously realized what was going on. Colton ripped open the back door and grabbed the hoodie.

"You've got to be kidding me," he said. A backpack

fell out of the bottom of the sweater, having been used to prop it up in the seat. Looking at the front passenger seat, he saw the same thing, a backpack stuffed into the hoodie, keeping it upright behind the seatbelt.

Chet's eyes were wide with horror. "Do you realize what you've done? Do you know what's at stake here?"

"I do. A young woman's life," she said curtly.

"It's more than that, Amelia," he said, dumbfounded. "You've just cursed an entire civilization."

PART THREE

PALO DURO: A THRILLER

CHAPTER TWENTY FOUR

RICKY AND JORDAN emerged from the cave and into the night air. Cicadas buzzed in trees all around them, a hum filling the otherwise quiet of the night. Ricky realized it was also much warmer than it had been when they'd entered the cave, and as a breeze blew in from the south, he knew. More a feeling, an intuition, but the difference in the cold early spring night they'd left and what they'd stepped out into now, he knew.

This wasn't their time. They'd found the portal and crossed the time rift to some other, ancient period. For a moment, he reveled in that thought. Of course, he'd studied Hawking and read about Einstein-Rosen wormholes. There was a part of him that, in the back of his mind, always doubted its possibility. That wormholes were science fiction. It was the workings of the human brain that imagined these possibilities. But perhaps there was a reason that time travel was a human fascination.

Because it *was* possible.

And now, standing in the open air of the canyon, he knew that he was centuries away from home. He felt validated. As insane as it had sounded when he'd seen the pictures uploaded from Rachel's phone, he knew that it was the only explanation.

Jordan stood beside him. "Are we?" she asked, not finishing her question, but looking all around.

"Yes, I think so," he answered.

The warm breeze felt great on his skin after having nearly frozen to death in the cold river. He could hear the water rushing somewhere nearby.

"Her pictures of the bison and the teepees weren't far from here," he said. "But I just realized I never got the coordinates of those from the metadata, so I don't know which way to go."

She started for the sound of the river. The vegetation around them was green and in full bloom, much more so than when they'd left. "Well, most of the time, Natives would set up their encampments near a body of water. Obviously, there's plenty of water flowing through the canyon, but I say we find the river and follow it. We're sure to run into someone soon."

The plan sounded plausible to Ricky, so he followed her to the river, the gurgling getting louder as they got closer. They approached the bank of the flowing water and stopped. Even in the dim light of the moon above, he could tell the water was clearer, cleaner. Ricky bent down and stuck his fingers in it.

"It's warm," he said.

"Would have been nice two hours ago," Jordan scoffed. "Let's follow it downstream, see what we come up with. We'll keep it quiet, though. Don't want to spook anyone."

"Lead the way," Ricky said. Next to the stream, there was little vegetation to push through or scrape past and it made the hike easy. Ricky actually enjoyed it, the warm air on his skin, the clear night sky.

And then it hit him. "Look at the sky," he said.

Jordan looked up. "It's stars."

"Exactly," he said. "With no satellites, planes or anything manmade. It's the sky the way it's meant to look." The constellations looked clear and distinctive. The Big Dipper and Little Dipper nearly straight above them in the unadulterated sky.

"Wow," she said, her eyebrows raised. "You just managed to sound more like Rachel than yourself."

"What can I say? This place is growing on me." He

stood for a few more seconds simply admiring the sky above them. He'd never seen anything so peaceful.

"Okay, starboy, let's keep moving," Jordan tugged on his sleeve and he continued to follow her.

"What if we do run into some tribe? Will they be hostile?" he asked, keeping his voice to just above a whisper.

"Probably," she said. "We are in the early morning hours, judging by the moon's position. But they will probably see that we are unarmed. If we do see anyone, keep your hands out to your sides. No sudden movements."

The thought of getting ambushed by a team of violent Natives didn't sound like a good time, but they hadn't seen any semblance or sign of civilization yet. In fact, the canyon looked entirely uninhabited, completely free of the manmade trails and signs that the park ranger service had erected in their time.

At their feet, little red flowers bloomed in bunches.

"Indian paintbrushes," Jordan said, noticing that he'd slowed down behind her to look at them. "They still have them in the canyon but they're not in bloom in our time."

"I wish it still looked like this, in our time," he said. "It's all so peaceful."

Ahead of them, a rustling sound in the brush made them both freeze. "Get down," Jordan commanded in a frightened whisper.

They ducked beneath the brushline, hugging close to the mesquite bushes. He didn't want to get back in the water, but worst-case scenario, Ricky figured they could jump into the river and hide if they needed to.

The rustling ahead of them continued and Ricky's heart began to beat faster. "Do we need to r—" he began, but they saw the figure come out of the brush and approach the water.

It was an animal, shaggy and brown, with a large hump behind its miniscule head. It looked like a baby, no taller than the two college students crouched next to the river.

"Is that a bison?" Ricky asked.

"Yes," Jordan answered. "A calf."

"Where's it's mother?" Ricky wondered aloud. He scanned the immediate area.

A heavier rustling in the bushes, coupled with trembling in the ground, made the color from Jordan's face drain. She turned to him, pale as a ghost and shoved him. Gripping his shirt collar, she stood up, pulling him with her. "Get up, get up," she panicked. "Run!"

CHAPTER TWENTY FIVE

AN ENORMOUS, HAIRY boulder crashed out of the mesquite bushes, charging directly toward them. The beast was so large and running at them that all Ricky saw was a massive brown blur. Both he and Jordan tried to get to their feet, but in their panic slipped in the muddy banks of the stream. The large animal rushed at them and Ricky grabbed Jordan, but it was too late. It hit her full force, knocking her back into the water.

Without thinking, Ricky jumped in after her and the bison stood at the water's edge, herding its calf behind it.

He pulled Jordan to him. Her body had fresh scrapes, superficial red scratches on her face and arms from where she'd hit some rocks in the stream. Her leg, however, was twisted in an unnatural and grotesque angle that made his stomach turn. He dragged her out of the water and pulled her to the opposite bank from the bison, which had decided to leave them alone and lumbered back into the wilderness.

"Jordan, wake up," he said as he gently shook the girl, trying to get her to show some sign of life. He felt for her pulse, pressing two fingers under the girl's jawline.

Finally, after what felt like a lifetime, she began to make sounds, coming back to consciousness.

"Careful, careful," Ricky said, holding her in his lap.

"What happened?" she moaned. Trying to sit up, she yelped in pain.

"Don't move. We got attacked by a buffalo," he said. "I'm going to try to get you up and take you back to the caves. We need to get some help."

"No," she protested. "We need to find Rachel. We don't know if the portal will even work again. And we have to leave while the moon is still full."

"Look at your leg, Jordan. We can't stay here. You need medical attention."

She looked down to see her leg twisted grotesquely just below the knee. She remained relatively calm despite wincing with pain. "It's okay. We can make a splint."

"What do you need?" he asked. She tried to sit up and he helped her lean against a boulder near the bank.

"Two sticks, about eight inches long and something to lash them with," she said, wincing as she pulled herself against the boulder, sitting up.

"Okay, I can do that. Are you going to be okay here by yourself?" he asked.

"Yes, but please hurry. We need to find Rachel and get out of here."

Ricky stood up and did an immediate scan of their surroundings. There was the river, of course, and behind them more brush and trees. The problem with the canyon was there wasn't a whole lot of large vegetation. Other than the mesquite bushes that dotted the canyon floor, there weren't many large trees from where he could gather the tools necessary for creating a splint.

Squinting, he could make out the silhouette of an outgrowth of trees off in the distance, probably no more than a mile from where they were now. His shoes were completely drenched from jumping into the river to save Jordan and water sloshed in them, but he started toward the trees. Before he left, he took Jordan by the hand.

"If you see anything, or if you are in danger, I want you to scream as loud as you can. I will run back," he said.

She nodded and squeezed his hand. "I'll be okay," she said.

With that, he began walking toward the trees, making his way through the brush. Unlike in their time, there weren't any trails and he kept his eyes open for the errant cactus on the ground that could stab him with its painful little needles.

After a few hundred yards away from the river, there was a trail, no wider than his own feet. It was much like the wearing down of dirt in the backyard where their dog back home in Decker would race up and down the fenceline. This seemed like something that had been worn over time, not necessarily built on purpose.

And then he remembered the teepees. In Rachel's photos, in the distance, there were teepees. Signs of civilization in the ancient canyon. He scanned the horizon once again, not seeing anything that resembled the images in her photographs. This little trail was a welcome respite from trudging through the overgrown brush.

He looked back over his shoulder to make sure he could still see the little clearing near the river where he'd left Jordan. He needed to find the components to make a brace for her broken leg, but perhaps they should wait until morning, if possible, to trek out to find Rachel or the teepees when there would be light from the sun above to guide him. Anything could happen in the dead of night. Hearing a coyote off in the distance, Ricky felt a sudden urge to turn back to her, to wait with her, when something else stopped him in his tracks.

A rustling of branches a few yards ahead made him freeze. He hoped it wasn't another bison. Or, something worse. Something with teeth. His biggest fear when Rachel had first went missing was that she was mauled and dragged off by some large animal like a mountain lion. Despite the evidence proving that to be false, only a figment of his imagination and paranoia, the idea of giant, dangerous creatures was still fresh in his head, no thanks to the attacking bison at the river.

Finally, his body catching up with his mind, Ricky started to backpedal and head to the riverbank where he'd left Jordan when a figure emerged from the thick brush.

It was a person. Young, like him, with dark skin and midnight black hair cropped short. He wore a brown tunic and not much else. The boy looked at him with amazement, said something that Ricky couldn't comprehend or understand, a collection of syllables that didn't form words in his mind, and turned to run away.

"Wait!" Ricky called out. "Wait, come back! I need help!"

He ran after the boy, continuously crying out,

ANDREW J BRANDT

"Come back! Please! We need help!" However, the stranger was fleet-footed and outran Ricky with ease. His side beneath his ribs aching from the exertion, Ricky slowed and eventually stopped running, his chest heaving, sucking in oxygen.

Once more he pleaded, speaking to the darkness, "Please. We need help. My friend is hurt."

Without warning, three men stepped out of the shadows around him, silently, without even so much as making sound to breathe. Unlike the boy, they were tall, handsomely built, with muscles that etched every part of their lean bodies. They wore little more than cloths to cover their private parts and two of them held weapons of sharpened bone at their side.

Ricky knew he was in trouble. One of the men moved in a blur directly in front of him and threw him to the ground. "Please, don't hurt me!" he screamed, covering his face defensively with his hands. "I need help!"

The man held the weapon high, the white bone shining under the full moon. A fourth person, however, softly spoke some unintelligible words. Despite not understanding what was said, he recognized the voice and, lowering his hands, opened his eyes.

The newcomer kneeled next to him and Ricky thought he was hallucinating. All this searching, months of insecurity and unanswered questions, all of it was embodied in this singular person. He'd gone from thinking he'd never see her again, to hoping against hope that she was still alive, to determined to find her when her phone had been discovered.

"Ricky," she said. "Why did you come here?"

CHAPTER TWENTY SIX

"RACHEL?" RICKY WAS stunned. Yet, here she was, clear as day. Her skin was darker than the last time he'd seen her. Her hair was adorned with a long feather that fell behind her ear. Creases formed in the corners of her eyes.

"Hi Ricky," she said. She then turned to the three men, holding a hand up and speaking to them again in that strange foreign language. They dropped their weapons to their sides and did something that astonished Ricky—they each took a knee and bowed to him.

"What's going on?" he asked, turning back to his sister. "Why are they bowing? How are you—" A well of emotion boiled to the surface and he began to cry.

Rachel wrapped her arms around him and held him for what felt like an eternity. Finally, able to collect himself, he continued, "How are you still here? Alive?"

"It's not been easy, at least not at first. But I adapted," she said. Taking him by the arms, she pulled him up off the ground, dusting him off. "You're all wet. Are you here alone?"

The three men stood at attention around them, unmoving and silent.

"No, actually," Ricky said. "Jordan is here with me. She needs help."

Rachel's expression changed to anger. "You *both* came through? Why? It's so dangerous. One of you could have been killed. There are mountain lions and bison and—"

Ricky cut her off, "Yeah, we met a bison. It attacked Jordan and she's near the river. Her leg is broken."

Rachel turned to her three guards, spoke again and they ran off in the brush, disappearing as quickly as they had arrived.

"Will you tell me what's going on?" Ricky asked.

"Take me to Jordan and I will," she said.

Ricky turned on the trail and led his sister back toward the river. "You look so different," he said, catching an occasional glimpse at her. Her body was much like that of the three men, sinewy yet muscular and lean. Her shoulders were wide, and she wore the same style clothing as they had; a brown tunic tied with a leather strap, like a toga except made of leather.

"It's been many moons," she said.

Ricky looked at her strangely and his twin sister cracked a smile. "I'm kidding," she said. "We don't actually talk like that. You should have seen your face though."

There it was. Her sarcasm and humor. Even if she looked different, she was still his sister.

"I think it's been close to three years," she said.

"What are you talking about?" he asked. "It's been four months."

"Four months in your—our—time," she said. "But once you go through the portal, it changes. You can stay here for months at a time and it would be a few days back in modern day."

"Why didn't you come back though?" he asked her. He felt something new in his gut, something like anger. "You've been alive this entire time, and you could have come back to tell us you were okay."

"I did, though," she said.

"When?"

"The phone, Ricky. I sent my phone back through. I didn't need it here. I etched my initials in it so you'd know it was me. I knew you would understand if I sent back a piece of technology."

"I've spent every day of the last four months wondering about you. Every single day, I never stopped thinking about you," he said curtly.

"I know. I thought it would be easier like this. To know that I'm okay, but that I wasn't coming back."

"Yeah, well, that's not the message we got," he huffed.

As they neared the river, she said, "We'll talk about this more once we get back home. For now, let's get her," she pointed to Jordan, who was propped against the boulder.

As they approached, the girl opened her eyes and did a double-take. Like Ricky, her eyes filled with tears that streamed down her cheeks. "No," she said. "It can't be. *Rachel?*"

"Hi, Jordan," Rachel said softly.

Jordan, forgetting about her leg in the moment, tried to stand, but grimaced in pain and let out a little yelp.

"Sit still, Jordan. Help is on the way," Rachel said.

"How did you find her?" Jordan turned to Ricky.

"I didn't. She found me," he said.

"A scout heard him in the mesquite," Rachel explained. "He was almost taken by my guards, but I could recognize his voice immediately."

"Your guards? I don't understand," Jordan said.

"From my tribe," Rachel said. "I know, it's a long

story. Let's get you back to the tribe and get your leg set. And then you two need to go back home, back to your time."

"Your time, too, Rach," Ricky interjected.

Rachel looked away, almost guiltily, and her eyes held a sadness that Ricky didn't quite comprehend.

The three men that had nearly killed him on the trail appeared out of nowhere again, this time carrying a kind of stretcher that looked to Ricky like it was made from hide and large branches. One of them handed Rachel a collection of sticks wrapped in leather straps. He bowed as he handed it to her, and she responded in kind.

"I'm going to brace your leg and then my guards will carry you back to our tribe," she said.

Jordan sat up as Rachel knelt next to her. "I'm going to have to set the bone back in place," she said. Reaching into a pouch on her tunic, she brandished a wad of leather coiled tightly. "It's going to hurt. Bite down on this," she instructed.

Jordan looked up at Ricky apprehensively and he knelt next to her and took her hand. She gripped it, her nails prodding into the skin between his knuckles as she placed the bit in her mouth.

"Breathe in," Rachel said. And, after a moment, "Breathe out."

As Jordan let her breath out, Rachel twisted the leg

and Jordan screamed.

"I know," Rachel said. "But you're good. I'm going to brace it now." They watched as Rachel unwrapped the planks from the leather strips and, placing them on either side of Jordan's broken leg, began to wrap the entire thing, starting high on her thigh above the knee and working her way down.

"It's very swollen," Rachel said as she finished up. "We need to get you back to the camp to get you some medicine."

Ricky said, "Why don't we just go back through the portal? Back to our time so we can get actual medical help?"

"Her leg could become infected. It will be impossible for her to walk out of the canyon. And she'd never make it. Her body could go into shock and she would die before you are able to get an ambulance down," Rachel said. "At least here we can give her medicine so she will survive the trip out of the canyon."

Rachel's silent guards stood at the ready, and when Rachel gave them a slight hand signal, they came to Jordan's side, lifted her carefully and placed her on the makeshift gurney.

Barking some order, they began to walk through the brush, one of the guards leading the way, with Rachel and Ricky tailing behind the two that carried Jordan. They walked through the canyon floor, finding another foot-worn trail in the brush.

The three men, who Ricky assumed were warriors in the tribe, glided gracefully on the trail, keeping Jordan steady on the stretcher. Their care and transport were much more skilled than Ricky could even hope to duplicate himself.

The far eastern horizon began to glow with the coming sunrise and Ricky was glad to finally be out of the darkness. As they trekked through the canyon, the sky began to glow in beautiful hues of reds and pinks. In the new morning light, he got a better glimpse of his sister. Her skin had become quite tanned in her time spent with this tribe.

Finally, they came through a clearing, through the trees that Ricky had spotted when Jordan first was injured, the tops of the teepees in the encampment sticking up, the support poles of each one interlocked. He'd of course seen images like the one in front of him from Rachel's books and studies over the years. Seeing it now, in person, was an entirely different experience. At one time, he couldn't imagine how a people could live without the things he worked with every day—it was difficult to even fathom a world without the technology that ran his modern life. Now, however, a peacefulness ran over him as he saw this place. Primitive, yes, but beautiful.

Several of the villagers came out of their teepees to

greet them. Their party was soon surrounded by a group of natives that had the same dark hair and mocha skin as the tribesmen who accompanied them.

A man, much older than many of the others, his long hair greying and tied in ponytails that hung at his ears, spoke to Rachel in the language that Ricky couldn't understand, though their body language told him that they were taking Jordan to one of the teepees for medical treatment.

Then, their conversation must have mentioned him, because the older man turned to him and, as Rachel spoke, nodded. Finally, as Jordan was led to the teepee, he approached Ricky, bowed, and said in broken English, "Welcome, brother of Princess."

CHAPTER TWENTY SEVEN

PRINCESS?! **DID HE** hear that right? Ricky cocked his head to Rachel who simply stood in place next to the elder.

The tribe elder continued, his English broken, "You must be weary. You, like the princess," he motioned to Rachel, "have come from a far away land."

All he could do was muster a simple "thank you" and bowed to the elder, who grabbed Ricky by the shoulder and led him to one of the teepees. Ricky saw that there were over a dozen of the dwellings, perhaps more, in the valley here. As they walked through the encampment, he saw women grinding what looked to him like grains and plants. Men were stripping the hides of some animal of the fat and sinew attached to it. Others were preparing baskets for fishing. On the backside of the teepees, Ricky saw rows and rows of plants, reminiscent of the backyard gardens their mother kept in Decker where she grew squash, tomatoes and other vegetables.

"Rachel, this is incredible," he said aloud, taking in all the hustle and bustle of the early morning routines of these people. Rachel, walking next to the elder ahead of him turned and winked.

They approached a teepee and the elder held the flap open for them while they stepped inside. The floor was dirt, packed hard, and a rug of what looked like bison hide was laid on top to provide a surface to sit. In the middle of the circular floor was a fire pit dug into the earth and surrounded by rocks.

"Sit," the elder motioned, and Rachel and he both sat in front of the pit. Despite no flames, the pit was warm, and Ricky assumed a fire had been lit the night before.

The elder and Rachel spoke animatedly and then Rachel turned to Ricky. "He says we will do what we can to nurse Jordan to health so that you can leave the canyon, but you must leave together."

The elder spoke again. Rachel translated, "Though you are the brother of the princess, you have not proven your worthiness of our tribe."

"Worthiness?" Ricky said. "Why do I care about being worthy? We didn't ask to be brought here!"

The elder continued talking, and Rachel again translated. "You have disturbed the Great Power of the Old Gods. You must prove your worthiness if you are to remain with the tribe."

"I don't want to remain with the tribe!" Ricky said. "I want to go back home, and I want you to come with me."

Rachel shook her head. Though the chief probably understood most of their conversation, he simply stared emotionless.

"I'm not coming back, Ricky. These are my people now. This is what I've always wanted. I've studied these tribes for years and I now get the opportunity to live with them. For my entire life, I've been searching for meaning, for a place I belong. And I have found it here."

"But what about mom?" Ricky asked. "You can't leave her wondering for the rest of her life what happened to you."

Rachel sighed. "I have learned to move on, to let go of the things that tie us to this earth. You must learn the same."

"That makes zero sense, Rach," he said.

The chief spoke, interrupting their terse conversation, and Rachel again translated, "You must leave by tomorrow. The people will be talking about you and Jordan, the strangers from a faraway land."

"Why do you get to stay though? You're from the same place we are. You must have disturbed the old god power or whatever it's called."

"Because I am a princess," she said. "And I earned my worthiness."

Another of the tribesmen came into the teepee. He was young and tall, his shoulders broad and rippling with muscles. He knelt to the elder, who stroked the newcomer's short hair. Then, turning to Rachel, he spoke to her in their tongue and she held her hand out—explaining, Ricky assumed—and motioned to Ricky.

The young man then turned to Ricky. "You are my brother. I am your brother," he said.

Ricky looked at him, confused. "My brother?"

Rachel took his hand. "Yes, Ricky. He is your brother. He is my husband."

"Wait—what?!" he asked, stupefied.

"In English, his name is Running Puma," Rachel said. "He is the son of the elder," she gestured to the old man sitting with them.

The younger native spoke to his father, who nodded and then spoke to Rachel. Ricky wished he knew what they were saying, but the language, made up of *ah*'s and *ko*'s and *toh*'s sounded completely foreign to him. At least he could understand some French, having grown up hearing their grandmother speak Spanish. He'd also learned some bits of Mandarin. This language, however, was nothing but unintelligible. He wondered how Rachel learned it so quickly, but then remembered she'd been here longer than the four months that she'd been missing in their time.

"To keep Jordan's leg from becoming infected and causing her to go septic, we need a root. We don't have it in the tribe, so we are going to have to find some," Rachel said. "I have volunteered you and me together to go find it and bring it back. If we do this, you will be seen as worthy of the tribe."

"What do I care if I'm worthy?" Ricky asked. "I can just go back to the present."

"These people—*my* people, Ricky—have risked their lives to bring you and Jordan back here," she said. "You owe them a life debt. Do not take that lightly. Now get up. We must find the root while the ground is still cool."

"And what? We're just going to leave Jordan here with them?" Ricky asked incredulously.

His sister, the princess of this tribe, turned to him with all the regality that came with her new title. "I trust them with my life. Now let's go."

CHAPTER TWENTY EIGHT

AFTER THEY'D TOLD Jordan where they were going, leaving her in the care of an older native woman with long gray hair tied back in a bun, Ricky and Rachel started into the canyon, toward the trees off in the distance. In what could only be described as the medical teepee, there were others on cots much like the one they'd transported Jordan on to the encampment. One, a young boy who couldn't be any older than twelve, had his arm in a sling; another, closer in age to Ricky and Jordan, was having a wound on his ribs bandaged and cleaned by a youthful female.

The sun was still low in the eastern horizon, but it was warming up quickly. Ricky knew they wouldn't have much more than a couple of hours at most before the yellow orb was beating down on them.

"I have to ask," Rachel said, once they were far from the tribe, "why neither of you brought supplies."

"It's a long story," Ricky said, doing his best to keep up with his sister. Her steps were light on the ground and she had the same almost supernatural ability to glide along the ground instead of tramp across it like he did. "We originally had Dr. Errington with us, but the plans changed. She took our backpacks to help create a diversion."

"Seems irresponsible."

"Well, we didn't have much choice if we were going to come get you. I don't think we ever thought we'd need much more than the clothes on our back. This was supposed to be a rescue mission after all, not a day trip time travel expedition," he said. As they hiked, his breathing became heavier and Rachel slowed down so that he could stay with her.

"Your breathing is not even," she instructed. "Feel your body bring in the oxygen. Breathe on purpose, not as a response."

"You really feel at home here, don't you?" Ricky asked.

Rachel stopped for a moment, seemingly to process the question. "I do. These are my people now. This place is my home. I chose to study at the university here on purpose, to be close to the canyon, to discover and research the civilizations that called this place home long before we did. Now I am here."

"I can't believe you got married," he said. "That's...crazy."

"I've been here for a long time. This tribe, these people, they became my family. I was able to help them with things like medicine. I taught Running Puma some English and Spanish. They will need it when the Spaniards come," she explained.

It was hard for Ricky to comprehend that it had been four months for him—four months of wondering, of giving up hope only to find it again. For her, though, in this place, years had gone by and it showed in her body, on the way she moved through the vegetation in the canyon floor and the way she spoke.

The last time Ricky had seen his twin sister, she was talking to him excitedly about pictographs in some cave down in the canyon. Then she had still had that youthful glow of finding the unknown and the naivete that being twenty years old afforded them. Now, however, she was a regal young woman, the princess of a Native American tribe.

As they hiked, finding themselves under a canopy of green trees, the shade was a welcome relief from the rising sun. A small stream, no more than a few feet wide, cut through the forest and Rachel knelt next to the crystal-clear water, filling a bison skin bag. It was things like this that Ricky found enthralling; that she could be so accustomed to these nuances of living a life in the past.

She stood and handed him the water bag. "This is the cleanest, purest water there is," she said.

He took the bag from her, apprehensively at first, and put it to his lips. The water, cold and delicious, flowed down his throat, quenching his thirst. He realized he hadn't had anything to drink since he and Jordan arrived in the past.

"Not too much, Rick," Rachel said. "You'll get a cramp."

Ricky pulled the water from his lips and handed the bag to her. She took a few small sips herself and strung the bag across her hips.

"How much farther do we need to go?" he asked.

Walking ahead of him again, she said, "Not much longer."

"What exactly is it we're looking for?"

"A healing root."

Ricky furrowed his brow to her non-answer, "Right, but what *kind* of healing root? What plant is it?"

"I don't know what it's called in English, to be honest," she said. "I never studied plants, you know, and I wasn't a botanist."

"It's amazing how much these people know about the world without the technology we have in our time,"

Ricky said.

"Of course. Humans have been on this planet for thousands of years. It is egotistical to believe that humans before your time had no knowledge because they lacked computers," she said. "In fact, I would argue that I've learned more from the oral traditions of my tribe than I ever did through books. They know more about the stars and the movement of the planet than the Europeans do right now."

"That's incredible," he said.

"It really is," she said, continuing to walk ahead of him. The trees overhead were getting thicker, blocking out more and more sunlight. It was decidedly cool here under the canopy of branches and leaves. "We've always had such a Euro-centric education about the proliferation of information, but really, most Native tribes know more about disease, astronomy and mathematics than the English and Spanish do at the same time period."

"Do you see many other tribes in this area?" he asked.

"Oh yes. We trade with some others south of us and to the east. Furs and fish and wood from the more forested areas are important here," she said.

"Dr. Errington said that the tribes here were in constant war over the land," Ricky said.

"Oh, not at all," Rachel said. "It's very peaceful.

Wars won't come until well after the Europeans start enslaving the people and taking the land and the resources."

"When will that happen?"

"Well after we've gone," she said. Then, she waved her hand at him, "Here it is, we've found it." Dropping to her knees in the soft dirt, Rachel began to carefully scoop handfuls of soil away from a gathering of tiny plants.

Ricky dropped to his knees next to her. "So we just give her this root and she'll be okay?"

"We will need to boil it to extract the medicinal properties, but yes," she said, not taking her eyes off the work. After a few minutes of delicate digging, she reached into the soil and tugged on the roots, gently lifting them out of the ground without breaking the main root or its many arteries that jutted out from it. Finally, the entire root, with all those little tendrils, came out of the ground and Rachel cradled it in her hand.

"We must keep it damp so it doesn't dry out on the way back home," she said. "Hold this." She handed the root to Ricky and he stared at it, the brown and gray little thing cradled in his hands. It felt brittle in his careful grip and he wondered what, exactly, it was. If he ever had a question or was curious about something, he could always fire up his computer and research it.

Here, however, there was no way to do that, and as Rachel took the root and rolled it in a wet strip of leather, he felt a tinge of what could only be described as homesickness.

They walked out of the canopy of trees and the sun was already high in the sky, beating down on them with a midsummer heat. If the root needed to stay wet, he knew they would need to hurry back to camp. Ricky also hoped that Jordan was okay and being taken care of by Rachel's adopted people.

Lost in his thoughts, he barely noticed the blur in the dirt that whipped up toward them. A snake missed Rachel's ankle by mere inches as she side-stepped the attack.

"Do not move," she instructed.

A strange sound began emanating from the tail end of the snake, a high-pitch rattle.

"This is a test of your worthiness," Rachel whispered. Slowly reaching to her waist, she held out a weapon, a knife of some kind, with a bone handle and a blade that seemed cut from stone. "You must kill it."

Ricky grabbed the weapon and gulped.

CHAPTER TWENTY NINE

"**WHAT DO I** do?" Ricky whispered as the rattle-snake blocked their path on the foot trail.

"Grab a stick from the side of the trail. Hold it down near the head and cut it off. But be careful," she replied. "They can still bite after decapitation."

Ricky, slowly and carefully, reached down to his side and picked up a branch from the ground. The dried-out stick, a remnant from one of the mesquite bushes that littered the canyon floor, was just long enough for him to reach out and trap the serpent's head.

Ever slightly, he moved to the side of the snake as it hissed and rattled, its tail buzzing with fervor. Ricky's heart pounded in his chest and his palms were nearly dripping with a nervous sweat. Though Rachel was nearly on top of it, completely still, the snake had its eyes glued on Ricky, and its head lurched back to strike. In a lightning-quick stab, Ricky forced the stick down on the snake and it thrashed and coiled its body around it. "Now!" she commanded. "Cut it!"

Ricky got down on his knees, lifted the blade high and brought it down on the creature's head. It came off in one fluid motion, blood spurting from the decapitation. The body of the snake writhed on the ground, the muscles jerking its long body in unsteady convulsions.

"Don't touch the head," Rachel said as she pulled the dead body to her. It continued to wring and writhe until it finally flopped still and lifeless.

"What are we going to do with it?" Ricky asked.

"We are going to eat it," she said. Ricky's stomach turned. "And you will get to keep the tail. This shows that you are brave and will be revered by the tribe. You will be allowed to leave, back to the caves."

"Wait, what?" Ricky asked. "They weren't going to let us leave?"

Rachel sighed. "The caves are a sacred place, Ricky. To disturb the magic of the cave is a sin that few have been absolved of. I brought medicine and understanding to the tribe. If I hadn't proved my worthiness, I would have been enslaved. Now let's get back so we can give the root to Jordan."

With its muscles still twitching, Rachel draped the snake over his shoulders like a scarf and he followed her back to the teepees.

* * *

They returned to the encampment and the root was boiled for Jordan. Speaking in the language of the tribe, Rachel recounted their adventure to the chief and his son, her husband—Ricky still couldn't believe that his sister was married—who both nodded their appreciation as they sat on logs outside the largest teepee.

The chief put his hand on Ricky's shoulder and said, in English, "You are brave."

"Thank you," Ricky said.

The chief nodded again.

Rachel also turned to Ricky, "We are going to have a feast in your honor, and then you and Jordan must return to our—," she paused, catching herself, "your time."

He didn't know how to feel. He had wanted more than anything to find Rachel, to know that she was alive. And, he'd done that—he could go on the rest of his life knowing that his sister was okay. But, at the same time, he felt selfish. He didn't want to live the rest of *his* life separated from her.

Most likely sensing the unease in his eyes, Rachel

stood and offered her hand to him. "Come with me. We need to find you a tunic to wear for the feast."

He took her hand and followed her to one of the teepees. Once inside, she looked down at the ground and shuffled the dirt with her feet. Quietly said, "Look, Ricky, I know this is hard."

He cut her off, "Yes it is! It *is* hard, Rach. Do you know how many nights I've spent awake wondering where you were? If you were okay?"

Guilt flashed in her eyes and she averted her gaze from her brother's, but he continued, "And now, here you are. But I don't understand why you won't come back with us. Come back home." He realized that he had tears in his eyes. "It's not just me. It's mom. It's Jordan. Even Dr. Errington. She risked her career and life getting us to the cave."

Rachel, however, was silent, taking in her brother's tirade. Finally, she spoke up, "I know. I know it's been hard for you, and for mom. And, at first, I did everything I could to come back home, until I realized that *this* is what I've always wanted. *This* place is what I've dreamed of, ever since I was a little girl."

"I get that, I do, Rach. But, come home. You need to come home. Even if you choose to come back here, Mom needs to see you, to see that you're okay. At least do that, please? At least give Mom that closure."

She looked down again, and Ricky felt the guilt of

his words hitting home in his sister.

"Rachel. Look at me," he said.

She did.

"Come home."

CHAPTER THIRTY

THE FEAST WAS extravagant, with dancing and chanting warriors, their headdresses emblazoned with feathers and colorful beads around their necks. Jordan was able to stand with the help of a pair of makeshift crutches fashioned out of wood and leather, her leg wrapped tightly and secured in a brace.

Ricky and Rachel sat together in the common area around which the teepees were situated and they laughed and told stories together, with Rachel translating as much as she could to the tribe.

A large bonfire lit up the darkening twilight and six warriors came over to Ricky, creating a path for the tribe elder. He spoke to the tribe, and Rachel leaned in to Ricky, whispering the translation, "Your defeat of the snake that tried to prevent you from completing our quest today has shown you are a mighty warrior."

The elder then motioned for Ricky to stand and, looking at Rachel, who mouthed, "It's alright," he did so. The elder took a smoking bunch of herbs bundled together and, circling Ricky, chanted as he waved the herbs all over Ricky's body. The elder's headdress, made of eagle's feathers that flowed down to his shoulders, rustled as he did. Then, motioning the young man to kneel, he displayed a leather necklace, high above his head. The entire tribe made a sound similar to an *ooh* and the necklace was placed over Ricky's head, settling on his collarbones. The leather strap held the rattle of the snake that he'd killed.

The elder then held his hand out and Ricky took it. Lifting him off his knees, the elder spoke again and the tribe began chanting, louder and louder. Taking Ricky's hand, he raised it high in the air and the tribe cheered. Rachel was beaming as he turned back to her.

The chief spoke again, first to the six warriors and then to Rachel. She nodded. "It's time to go," she said.

Rachel's husband put his hands on Ricky's shoulders and investigated the rattlesnake necklace. Then, he turned to Rachel and hugged her. Ricky noticed he had tears in his eyes.

"So this is it? Just like that?" he asked as Rachel and her husband let go of each other.

"Yes. It is getting dark," she said.

The warriors gathered up the stretcher that had been used to transport Jordan through the wilderness the night before and laid it at her feet. With some help, she was placed on it and they lifted her up.

All around, the natives came up to Ricky and bowed to him, some offering him beads and bits of bone carvings as parting gifts. Children swarmed at his feet, their eyes wide with wonder as they grabbed at his knees and waist. He thanked them each, and was soon led by his sister and the warriors back on the trail toward the caves.

"I thought the people lived in the caves," he said.

"They are our holy place," Rachel replied. "We don't live in them, but we visit them when we need guidance. To speak with the gods, to our ancestors. Someday, they will be used as a fortress, but not for a very long time."

"You seem to know a lot about what's coming," he said.

She turned to him. "I do," she said, her tone blunt and serious.

"Listen," he quickened his pace to walk next to her, "about earlier, I just want you to know, I understand why you want to stay here."

"It's okay, Rick," she said. "You don't have to apologize."

"I know. I just wanted my sister back. But this experience, coming through that portal, and finding you here—it's more than I could have hoped for. Thank you for that," he said.

Rachel gave him a side glance and a smile. "You're welcome."

After nearly an hour, they reached the mouth of the caves, and the warriors leading their convoy slowly and carefully let Jordan down from her stretcher as one of them handed her the crutches. The warriors then bowed to the three of them and began making their way back toward the encampment, leaving them alone.

Rachel motioned to the caves. "I suggest you go first, Ricky, and then I will help Jordan through."

Jordan, who still looked rather groggy from her injury and the root serum she'd been given simply nodded her understanding. Ricky stepped into the cave and, as Jordan hobbled in, he grabbed her waist and she put an arm around him.

"I'm ready to see an actual doctor," she said with a loopy smile.

"I bet you are," he replied. "You'll get to very soon."

"No one is ever going to believe what happened here," she said.

"That's okay. They don't have to know," Ricky said.

He took Jordan's hand, and she laced her fingers between his.

From behind them, Rachel stepped through the entrance of the cave and said, "Will you two stop flirting and get out of the way?"

"Wait," Ricky said, confused. "What are you doing?"

"I'm coming back with you." Rachel smiled, tears beginning to form in her eyes. "You said it yourself. I need to come back home. Even if it's not forever."

Ricky was stunned and started to speak, but Rachel hushed him with a gentle touch. Her palm, calloused from living here, caressed his cheek. "Mom deserves to know what happened. There are people back home who need answers, and I need to give them those answers."

Ricky nodded his understanding. Then, together, with Jordan, they walked through the portal.

CHAPTER THIRTY ONE

THE THREE OF them stepped through the cave and out the opposite end. The night air was cooler, and Ricky felt Jordan shivering next to him as she hobbled out into the open air.

To be certain that he wasn't dreaming or hallucinating, he turned and Rachel was still right behind them. He couldn't help himself as he pulled her in and wrapped his arms around her. Letting go of her, he looked at his watch. The LCD display read a time that confused him.

"It's twenty minutes off from when we first came in," he said. "I think that we've only been gone for twenty minutes in this time."

Jordan hobbled a bit more to a rock that would support her and she sat on it. "I think you should go find us some help," she said.

Rachel agreed and Ricky started down the path from the caves toward the boulder garden trail. Within ten minutes, he was on the trail and making his way to the trailhead where he hoped to find a park ranger who he could have call in some backup. He knew that, even with the herb and root medicines that Jordan had been given by the Native tribe, she would need actual, modern medical attention for her broken leg.

He walked along the trail, ducking under a string of yellow police tape that had been weathered to the point of nearly fraying. As he reached the trailhead, he saw a pair of headlights coming his way, with perfect timing. He figured it was one of the park rangers making the rounds on the trails.

Waving his hands high above his head to get the park ranger's attention, the truck pulled into the parking area, and the ranger got out. Ricky gulped. It was Chet Smallbone.

"Oh no," he muttered.

Colton stepped out of the passenger seat, and behind him, Dr. Errington emerged from the backseat.

"Good, looks like we caught up to them before they went in the caves," Smallbone announced.

"No, we're back," said Ricky. "We're back from the

caves. We need help, though. Jordan's hurt."

"Wait—you…" Smallbone trailed off, his eyes wide and looking back toward the direction of the caves.

"Yes. We went through," Ricky said. "But, please. She really needs help. Her leg is broken. Got trampled by a bison."

They all looked dumbfounded, not quite understanding the words that he spoke. Finally, he waved them on as he started back down the trail, "What are you waiting for? Come on!"

As they hastily made their way down the trail, Chet Smallbone radioed in for an ambulance. The two rangers and Dr. Errington followed Ricky and he led them back to the caves, where Jordan and Rachel sat, waiting for them.

Dr. Errington saw Rachel first and gasped. "Oh my god, is that—"

Rachel approached her, "It is," she said.

The professor broke down and embraced her student. "I never thought we'd see you again," she sobbed. She held Rachel out at arm's length, taking her in. "You have to tell me *everything*."

"I will. There's so much to know," Rachel said.

"You all made it back through," Smallbone said disbelievingly. "That's never happened."

"Well, sir," Ricky said, "we had a lot of help. On this side and the other."

Colton approached Jordan and kneeled next to her, the girl's leg sticking straight out on the dirt. "I am so sorry," he told her. "I hope you can understand that I have a job to do."

"I do," she said. "And I hope you understand that we're over."

As they waited for the emergency responders to arrive at the trailhead, Chet Smallbone gathered them all together.

"Look," he said, averting his eyes from their collective gaze. "I want to apologize for my actions, for keeping you from this place. My people have been the guardians of this holy site for generations."

"It's okay, Chet," Dr. Errington said. She nodded to the students. "This cave will remain a secret."

Ricky, Jordan and Rachel all nodded in agreement. Ricky spoke up, "I understand that you thought what you were doing was best, but I couldn't not try to find her."

"And I'm glad you did," Smallbone said. "But this place cannot be disturbed again. The power is too volatile."

Under the light of the full moon, they all swore to secrecy, that the cave and its power would remain guarded by all of them for as long as they all lived.

* * *

Jordan had been transported out of the canyon by ambulance to a hospital where she could get medical attention for her broken leg. Ricky and Rachel sat in another ambulance, both of them being examined and prodded by the emergency responders.

"I'm fine, I'm fine," Ricky protested as they checked his temperature and blood pressure. "Hey," he called out, "Doctor Errington?"

The professor came to the open hatch of the ambulance.

"Can you grab my backpack?" he asked. "I need my phone."

The woman left and returned, handing him the device. He turned it on and scrolled through his contacts. He pressed the button to call and held the phone to his ear.

After a few rings, the call connected.

"Hello?" the speaker on the other end said. "Ricky?"

"Hey, mom," he said. "I, uh," he started, taking a moment to gather his thoughts and make them make sense. "Well, I have some good news. But, someone else should tell you."

He handed the phone to Rachel. She looked at it

apprehensively, and then held it to her ear, "Hi, mom," she said. "It's me. It's Rachel."

EPILOGUE

RICKY HEARD A faint sound in the darkness of his dorm room, almost like a scratching, and he opened his eyes. His bedside clock read 8:30. He couldn't remember the last time he was up this early. Final exams would commence that week, and he was looking forward to sleeping in today before packing his things to go back home to Decker for the summer. It would be the last summer before graduation.

He looked around his room for the source of the sound that awoke him, but everything seemed to be in order. Then he saw it, the envelope that had been slid beneath the door.

He crossed the miniscule dorm room, picking it up.

Flipping on the light switch next to the door, the overhead light blazed in a harsh white glow and he blinked a couple of times to adjust to the new brightness.

The white envelope had his name written in a scratchy, ineloquent hand, and he knew immediately who it belonged to. He'd made fun of her handwriting for years. Tearing open the envelope, he began to read.

Ricky,

I am going back. Thank you for convincing me to come back to tie up loose ends, especially with mom. She already knows about my choice to go. I can never thank you enough for the love you've shown me. I will always think of you. You are the most intelligent person I have ever known.

Love, through all time,
Rachel

P.S. - I think you'll find something interesting in the cave. Also, take care of Jordan. And, if I were you, I'd ask her out. I have it on good faith that she would say yes.

He held the letter in his hands, reading it over a couple of times, smiling, crying and laughing. He'd feared that this would happen, that she would choose to go back, but he couldn't blame her. Like she'd told him, it was what she'd always wanted, always dreamed of.

The last line stood out to him. *Something interesting in the cave*? What could that mean?

Within thirty minutes, he was dressed and in his vehicle—Rachel's hand-me-down Subaru—and driving out to the canyon. The letter was in the passenger seat, unfolded. He left the radio off, preferring to drive in silence. At the entrance to the state park, he paid the fee and drove down into the canyon.

At the boulder garden, he parked at the trailhead and started hiking. Beads of sweat formed in his hairline and dripped down the sides of his face as he walked, trudging on the path that lead up through the boulder gardens. Taking the fork that led off the main trail, he ducked under the barbed fence and continued on.

Finally, he saw it. The cave ahead of him. He entered, the cool and damp air inside a welcome change from the heat of the cloudless early May morning outside. He remembered just like it was yesterday, the path through the caves that led to the little slit that hid the chamber of cave drawings.

He slipped through the opening and found himself there again, staring at all those ancient drawings, in red and black, outlined in gold. One caught his eye, though.

In the bottom corner, he saw something that wasn't there the first time. Using the flash on his phone as a light, he approached the wall, examining the carvings.

There were stick figures carrying another on a platform above their heads. Behind them, another character, a crown above his head and a snake around his shoulders. He couldn't help but smile as he ran his fingers over the drawings. He could have stayed there all day, remembering their adventure with the tribe.

Standing up, Ricky dusted his hands off on his pants and went back through the caves and out the way he came. The warm late spring sun met him with a comforting brightness. Starting back on the dirt trail to his vehicle, he looked forward to getting back to campus. He had a girl to ask out on a date.

THE END

SPECIAL ACKNOWLEDGEMENTS

If you've gotten this far, it means you finished reading *Palo Duro*. Thank you for reading this book. This one is really special to me, because as much as it is a fun mystery adventure story, it's a love letter to my home. I spent many weekends while attending West Texas A&M University as a twenty-something young man down in Palo Duro Canyon. There's a magic to that place that you just have to feel in person.

I have a lot of people to thank in this section. When the pre-order for *Palo Duro* was announced, everyone who pre-ordered the paperback before a specific date would have their name listed in this section. If you see your name here, just know that you are appreciated beyond measure. Not only do the pre-orders help with Day 1 sales (incredibly important in this industry), but we also pledged a portion of the proceeds from every pre-order to Storybridge, a nonprofit organization in Amarillo, TX that provides books to underprivileged children in the Texas panhandle. As of this writing, Chandra Perkins and her team at Storybridge have given over one hundred thousand books to those deserving kids. I am so excited that we, you and me, Dear Reader, get to add to that number.

First, to Jennifer. You are the consummate partner and my best friend. Thank you for supporting this endeavor. Thank you for reading every book and for listening as I ramble about my story and character ideas. I love you.

Derek Porterfield — I thanked you in *In The Fog*, and then you mentioned me in the Acknowledgements of *No-Mod: Book 1 of the Mute-Cat Chronicles*. So, I feel it necessary to once again list you in these pages. Thank you, and you're welcome, and thank you.

Brandon Biggers — Thank you for taking on the project of editing these books. Thank you for helping me shape these ideas into stories and for being a sounding board. They wouldn't be what they are without your careful eye.

Danielle Girard and Rick Treon — thank you both for beta reading this story well before it was completed and for the feedback. Thank you for lending your names and your blurbs to the cover. And, Rick, I'm sorry I had to bump you for Danielle.

To everyone who pre-ordered this book, thank you:

Gabe Morgan
Andrew Monroe
Kenny Nagunst
Niccole Caan
Nicole Reeves
Betty Whitfield
Trey Liles
Nikki Barrett
Michele Lester
Kristi Asplof
Kristin Anderson
Carla Defrance
Teresa Brewer
Joyceanne Willis
Malinda Riggins
Bonnie Ballos

Sherry Philyaw
BJ Swatzell
Mark Hopkins
Karon Anderson
Abby Jimenez
Cheryl Estill
Amy Piercy
Jane Mitchell
Kandace Aliff
Lyssa Kay Adams
Holly Stone
Nicole Moore
Leslie Supina
Charles D'Amico
Marco Munoz
Suzann Dykhouse

ANDREW J BRANDT

Melynda Henson
Beth Cameron
Joanne Wells
Gaye Henry
Amy Macrander
Courtney Aliff
Susie Knippers
Suzanne Gochenouer
Audrey Glenn
Jeremiah Cunningham

Raphael McHenry
Warren Aliff
Gayle Neusch
Dr. Regina Parks
Donna Sherrod
Aaron Peckham
Elizabeth Martin
Carol Mead
Elizabeth Williams

ABOUT THE AUTHOR

Andrew J Brandt is a graduate of West Texas A&M University and the author of multiple bestsellers, including the #1 young adult thriller *The Treehouse*. In theory, he is writing his next novel. In reality, however, he is on the patio with a beer and watching the Chicago Cubs.

Andrew resides in Texas with his wife and children.

For more information, follow Andrew J Brandt on Facebook at facebook.com/writerbrandt or on Instagram at @writerbrandt.

Subscribe to his newsletter and purchase autographed paperback books and other products at his website www.writerbrandt.com.